Stringer

by Ward Just

Stringer

Ward Just

An Atlantic Monthly Press Book

Little, Brown and Company — Boston — Toronto

To Ben Bradlee and Robert Manning

Library of Congress Cataloging in Publication Data

Just, Ward S
  Stringer.

  "An Atlantic Monthly Press book."
  I. Title.
PZ4.J97St [PS3560.U75]   813'.5'4   73-13682
ISBN 0-316-47721-4

ATLANTIC—LITTLE, BROWN BOOKS

ARE PUBLISHED BY

LITTLE, BROWN AND COMPANY

IN ASSOCIATION WITH

THE ATLANTIC MONTHLY PRESS

Published simultaneously in Canada by Little, Brown & Company
(Canada) Limited

PRINTED IN THE UNITED STATES OF AMERICA

Stringer

one

THERE WAS just himself and one other, and the high mountain in front of them. It was not a difficult mountain, and no experienced climber would regard it as any sort of challenge. But it was massive and revealed itself gradually as they moved up the slope; the glittering countryside lay motionless around them. They had found this mountain after three days of searching. Mountain Number 1375, according to the map that they had; the number represented the height in meters. It was gentle at the base and steep at the top, and an uncertain trail wound through its deep underbrush and dense rock outcroppings. In the mornings the clouds cleared and patches of blue were visible in the direction of the summit. He and Price hiked carefully in tandem, keeping to the edges of the narrow path. The fields rose in a ground swell, their slopes packed with the usual wild flowers. He plucked a flower that looked like a daffodil and put it in his buttonhole. Price disapproved.

The big river was far behind them now, hidden as they moved into smaller valleys and emerging again as they came out onto the heights. The closer they got, the more forbidding the mountain: gray and angular in color and shape, a dark cloud perched like a fedora at the summit. The mountain's rocks vaulted up and out of the heavy grass and underbrush. They saw no living thing except for the birds, hawks drifting high. Inland, away from the river, there were no people. It was as if the air and the land were poisoned: the people clung to the riverbanks. He and Price agreed not to talk as they stepped up the slope.

Later, thirsty and tired, they sat on the high side of a hillock and took ten minutes' rest. He unhooked a shatterproof bottle from his belt and poured the last of his limeade, the smell of it overpowering the sweet smell of grass. He lit a cigarette and watched the smoke blow away with a rush. He patted his stomach and put the limeade on the ground beside him and took out a piece of chocolate and began to eat it. The tastes mingled in his mouth, the chocolate, the limeade and the cigarette with the smell of the fields. Friends getting acquainted. This was excessive, and he laughed out loud.

"What's funny?"

He was watching the land fall away, loving the descending curves. He thought it was massive yet delicate, the land precise in its definition. He felt a light breeze and did not reply right away.

"What's funny?" Price barked again.

"It's so damned pleasant."

Price grunted and looked away.

"It's not so bad here, if you can get high enough. Nice roll to the land, Price."

The other one was standing now, silent, looking around him through the binoculars.

"Heads up, Price." He laughed and field-stripped his cigarette, tucking it under a rock, a small offering. He'd field-stripped cigarettes for as long as he could remember. Now he had a scattered cigarette and a half-eaten bar of chocolate and the limeade. He figured if he concentrated imaginatively, he could manage those two and the sight of the landscape. The landscape was nowhere reminiscent of any other, even the shades of green were unfamiliar. Price had already collected his gear and was impatient to go.

"Well, let's move. What are you waiting for?"

"Fuck you, Stringer."

He laughed, and they moved off the rock. The sunlight was hazy through the disappearing clouds, but the day was warm. Listening, he heard the sound of insects in the grass and of wind. He was sorry now that he hadn't stripped his pack to the barest of essentials, but he was superstitious about the pack. Sweet-smelling air filled his head, and he gazed at the hills below him and the minute shimmer of water beyond them. He saw the empty village and the road cutting through it. He looked at his watch, it was noon; on schedule. Shading his eyes, Stringer stared at the summit and the hill seemed less forbidding. Although it rose steeply, the rocks thrusting up here and there, the hill was not ominous or menacing. Up another two hundred yards the grass stopped altogether, choked off by rocks. There they would begin the traverse, a switchback, moving up the mountain in a slow swing, taking half a dozen strides sideways for every stride forward. The view of the countryside was already magnificent, and he decided that the climb was worth it, even if it was necessary. The shoes with their thick soles encouraged him to believe that he was taller than he was, and standing on the stones he felt huge, a giant. Gulliver, God, looking down at the soft land, indistinct now.

"Your turn," Price said. Stringer halted and shucked his own pack and accepted Price's. Now he had twenty pounds more weight to carry, and he could feel the tension in his back and spine. They began climbing again.

He heard Price behind him, breathing hard. The trail was steeper now, rocks the size of houses stuck out from the side of the mountain. The summit was lost to his view, and the way up more complicated and confusing. It unsettled him to look down now, he had never been good with heights. He understood what climbers meant when they talked of handling a mountain, working with it instead of against it. The mass became animate, a personal intimate thing. Once he slipped and glided down the slope a few feet, the length of his body in touch with smooth rocks; he felt as if he were sliding down a stone mattress, a forty-pound pillow on his back. He'd let himself go, moving with the mountain, sagging and falling with it; then his foot caught a ledge and he pulled himself up again, still feeling part of it, his shoes glued to the stone face.

Trembling with exertion, he concentrated on technique, the manner of movement, the climb itself. Move with economy, conserve your strength; palms flat out against the stone, feet working slowly and smoothly, all of it done with care and caution, in rhythm. And certain knowledge, the confidence of experience. He was made aware of his arms and legs, and the punishment of bone and muscle, and his own sense of control.

They were below a large overhanging rock now, slipping sideways to move around it in order to climb. A quick glance down showed him their mistake; they'd taken what seemed to be the natural route, gone left instead of right, the wrong turning at the wrong rock. But there was no way of knowing that, looking up altered the perspective and therefore the nature of the terrain. Looking down, the trail seemed very small and oddly positioned. That was the wonderful thing about hindsight, it was morbid; no optimism in hindsight. The thing that history taught was more history. It had no other application. He kept his head into the mountain, working with it, moving sideways until he could move no more. The ledge bumped into another barrier, and they were at a dead end.

Two hawks crisscrossed above them, a curvy double X, riding wind currents, silent as the mountain itself. He looked straight ahead at the green-veined stones, staring at them the way a fortune-teller stares at the lines in a man's palm. He watched the birds from the corners of

7

his eyes, the birds' black skins silhouetted against a milky daytime moon, fastened to the sky like a button.

He heard Price behind him, unpacking the equipment. A breeze drifted down the mountain and dried the sweat on his head. He turned to watch Price with his hammer and pitons and length of rope. He was whistling softly, absorbed in the equipment. He spread it all out, just so, on the ledge. This was well-worn equipment, very light and carefully packed.

"Quiet," Stringer said.

"As possible," replied Price.

"You go first," Stringer said.

"Right. I'll go first, you second with the big pack. I'll send down a rope. You can use the rope and the pitons, no sweat."

Price set to work, hammering the pitons. He was big, bigger than Stringer and younger by about six years; Price's big head was bent toward the equipment. He would need only three or four pitons. Price completed his work swiftly and efficiently, and fifteen minutes later they'd scaled the rock face and were standing on a bluff leading to the summit. There were no flowers now, just dwarf shrubs and heavy gorse. While Price gathered his kit, Stringer scouted the mountain: up, down, long looks to the left and right, a careful inspection of their surroundings. He was looking for any sign of trespass, a cigarette pack, the residue of a fire, paper of any kind. There was nothing at all, the bluff was pristine.

"What do you see, Stringer?"

"The footprints of a gigantic hound," he muttered.

"What the hell are you talking about?"

"A joke, Price."

"Well, you can save those."

"There's nothing here. No hounds, no nothing."

"Save the jokes." Stringer waited for him to say it again, Price valued repetition. "Forget the jokes and let's move out," Price said.

That was a reminder that although they were theoretically equals, Price was in charge. Nominal charge. Price's abilities had given him a dramatic manner, he appeared to be a man who lived through his performance, a man in a mirror. Price was a man without doubt as some Spanish are said to be *sin vergüenza,* without shame. Stringer thought that Price belonged, really, to another century. Another century in another country, although the line of work would be the same. It was pleasant enough working with Price because in the daytime and at dusk Stringer could relax and read a book and depend on Price not to interrupt him with casual conversation; there was nothing casual or offhand about Price. The inspection completed, they moved rapidly toward the summit, lurching a little under their heavy loads. They found a wide place under a large rock and put the packs down. Then they shouldered their rifles and without a word moved off in opposite directions to reconnoiter the summit.

It was inauspicious country, the loneliest that Stringer had ever seen. The top of the mountain was the size and shape of a football field, filled with boulders and tilted at crazy angles. The panorama was grandiose: below him was a valley and beyond that a mountain chain that rippled away to the west. This was uninhabited high ground, the ridges rising to meet the massif fifty miles away. There were half a dozen ridges, the nearest dark purple and the others giving way to blue and finally light gray. The colors changed with the position of the sun. In front of him and down was the road running north and south, barely visible with the naked eye. A breeze swirled round the summit, cool and humid and welcome.

Their maps were in error, as they always were: Mountain Number 1375 was about two hundred meters off in height and positioned incorrectly. The northeast corner of the summit was a cone-shaped pulpit, which gave them a view not only of the approaches but of the objective itself. That was the road that wound through the valley. Stringer and Price meticulously moved around the summit, looking for signs of habitation. There were none, only the dusty droppings of animals, probably deer. The place could easily be mistaken for a sportsman's paradise — and in a way, that was what it was. By three in the afternoon, they had their equipment, the scopes and the radio transmitter, tucked away from view. There were two scopes, big, German-made long-throated telescopes protected by chamois cloth, which they kept trained on the northern approach to the road.

They took their time focusing the scopes and inspecting the valley.

"Empty," Price said.

"Absolutely."

"You might as well go now to plant the box."

"Yes."

"Within twenty yards of the road," Price said. It was half statement, half order.

"Right," Stringer answered. He was looking down the slope, not listening to Price.

"Remember the antennae."

"Anything else, Price?"

"When there is, you'll be the first to know."

Stringer let it pass. He was worried about the road, and the routes to it. Without the weight of the radio or the backpack he could move down the mountain to the road in two hours. It would take him three hours, more or less, for the return. He reflected again that the central qualification for his job was stamina: Stringer could run all day, if required. Two hours down and three hours back would bring it to eight o'clock. Still an hour of daylight, sufficient margin. He put his rifle with the rest of the gear, there was no reason to take it. He strapped on his pistol and put the small black box in his shirt. Stringer took one last look around and was gone, disappeared over the edge, moving down the mountain slope to the road.

He followed an overgrown path, looking back frequently. He didn't want to lose his orientation, which was easy to do in unfamiliar surroundings. He moved very quickly, stepping lightly and carefully over tree roots in the middle of the path. This was strange territory, half jungle and half forest; the forested parts were dark, no sun penetrated the canopy. There was nothing to distinguish this particular forest, yet it was like no other he'd ever seen; the air was charged with a devout silence. The path appeared to be an animal path, there

11

were no signs of human footprints. He moved swiftly and was barely out of breath when he arrived at the ditch near the road. It took him a moment to understand that it was not a ditch at all, but an old bomb crater overgrown with vegetation.

He lay very still for a moment and listened; no sound. He took the black box from his pocket and switched it on, pulling the antennae as he did so. He put the box to his ear but could hear nothing; the thing was the size and shape of a cigarette pack but weighed about two pounds. A modern marvel of technology, the surface smooth and silky, dull. It had a dangerous, expensive feel to it because it was heavy and small, smooth and black, like a jewel case. Stringer laid it on the ground and covered it with grass and leaves and then, still peering cautiously around him, moved very slowly closer to the road itself. He stumbled once and almost fell into a second crater, entirely concealed by the deep underbrush. Along the edges of the road were cartons and water flasks, and the surface itself had been deeply rutted by tracked and wheeled vehicles. He closely inspected one of the tracks and decided that it bore the signature of a tank, one of their small models. This was a heavily traveled road, no doubt about that. It was no doubt exactly what they said it was, an important supply route.

Stringer remained perfectly still, listening. He heard nothing except insects, and then he exhaled and a moment later was making his way back to the camp at the summit of the mountain. The convoys would come at night, their headlights shrouded. He and Price would hear nothing, and see nothing until the box began to click and transmit its message; then with the help of the scopes they might see tiny pinpricks of light along the road. He wanted to sleep before the night's work, so he made haste up the path.

At eight sharp he joined Price, who was sullenly eating his dinner, staring fixedly at the road. Price had put the food and water at the base of the rock and wordlessly indicated it. There. Eat. Stringer shook his head, he decided he wouldn't eat just then. Steinberg would've remembered the flask of vodka, and now they'd be bent over the magnetized board playing bad chess. But not Price. Price was all business. Stringer took a worn paperback from his pocket and riffled the pages. The book was soggy, the paper stuck together; he always had it with him. This was a book by a writer who had journeyed to Africa to escape — what? — boredom. The writer wasn't precise about his motives, although Stringer thought he understood them. Stringer read a page, then put the book down. In fifteen minutes he was asleep, his head on his chest, facing the sun.

He snapped awake and slid to the right. He felt his eyes blinking, he wasn't sure where he was. He'd been dreaming, but the dream was gone. It was nearly dark, the sun's rays failing over the mountain ridge, spilling a dark green light in the valley. He scrambled to the lip and looked over it and down: perfect silence, nothing. The road was almost invisible in the half light, easily missed if one did not know it was there.

"Stringer?" Price was adjusting the radio, correcting the dials. Stringer looked at Price, bulky in his black

13

clothing, and decided that even when squatting he was at attention. Price turned off the radio and swung around to look at him. "They expect some movement tonight."

"They called?"

"They did. Just signed off."

"Some movement, is it? That's what they said the last time."

"This is this time."

"Last time they said it was the heaviest convoy since Napoleon marched into Russia. Trucks, half-tracks, tanks, personnel carriers, a mobile command post, troops, the works. They even had a name and a number for the regiment, where it had trained, where it was headed. So they said, 'Get your ass on up to blah-blah-blah' — I forget the place. To find not a damned thing." Stringer smiled sourly. In a week of observation a month ago they'd seen two men, both old, riding bicycles. So he and Steinberg had argued whether to call in a strike on the two old men on bicycles. It was a puzzle to him even now whether Steinberg was serious. He *appeared* serious, but with Steinberg you didn't always know. The two old men were either couriers or tourists, Steinberg said, and everyone knew the tourist season was at its peak. Warm days, cool nights. Never a cloud in the sky. In the end they didn't call in the strike because it would have been easy to evade and a waste of money. Steinberg, in the end, was cost-conscious.

"It's good intel," Price insisted.

"Sure it is. I'll believe it when I see it."

Price was lost in thought, a bad sign. Price's thoughts tended to be elaborate, or at least difficult. He was at pains to improve the odds and was a bear for technology. A very modern man in that respect, a man who understood the uses of machines, and who could put the machines in the service of men. No small achievement. Price was at home with gear, watches rifles transmitters knives. At headquarters, he was proud that everything he wore was regular army issue — from his boots to his dog tags. Price sat quietly now, clicking his thumbnail against his front teeth. Stringer began to eat a chocolate bar.

"I've been thinking, while you were asleep. I think we ought to plant another box, farther up the valley. Closer to the northern approach. At these coordinates." Stringer leaned over Price's shoulder, looking at the point where his finger touched a whorl on the map. Then he looked up to fix the place in the valley. It appeared to be about a mile north of the first box.

"Why?"

"Insurance."

Price's point was well taken. Stringer knew he'd moved too hastily. They had four boxes in all, one other could be easily spared. "It makes some sense," he said agreeably.

"I think so."

"A hell of a long walk."

Price sneered. "You're up to it, Stringer. I can tell."

"When do they expect the convoy?"

"Right away. Tonight."

"Well, there's no way in hell to plant that box now. It's too late. I'll go at first light."

Price, smiling: "Not to worry, Stringer. Not to worry. You can do it in the morning, at your leisure. No sweat there. Not to worry, not to hurry."

Stringer looked at him a long minute. Then he said resignedly, "Do you want the first watch?"

"Yes."

Stringer ate a tin of chopped beef and drank half a cup of water and tried to sleep. He used his pack for a pillow, his poncho for a blanket. When the moon rose, their laager was lit bright as day. He tried to fall asleep thinking about women, first one woman, then another. But it didn't take, it never did. He positioned them in exotic surroundings, parading them in his mind's eye seconds apart, like a talent scout at an audition. They were self-possessed women, young, well-shaped, sensual, innocent. But he was unable to concentrate, his mind wandered back to the valley and to Price, and the mission itself. Price and his obsession with *things*. He rolled over, his eyes squeezed shut against the moonlight. At length he slept and dreamed of an elegant banquet. The banquet was held on board ship, and when it was time to leave the host presented him with a large bill. He pulled a wallet from his pocket and found it stuffed with bank notes, but they were all Xerox facsimiles. He smiled apologies at the host — so sorry! — but the host only turned away, disappointed. He stood on the ship's gang-plank in his tuxedo with a fistful of Xerox money, a woman's hand on his shoulder. She was shaking him by the shoulder, and then he woke. It was Price. Two A.M., his watch. Price was very punctual and wasted no time with conversation. He tapped Stringer twice, then went back to his own pack and flopped down and went to sleep. Stringer watched him sourly. Price slept at attention, undisturbed by either dream or nightmare.

Stringer took the binoculars and went to the top of the rock, where Price'd been. He began at the south end of the road and swept north. They were remarkable glasses, not as powerful as the telescopes, but designed for darkness, acquiring light from the stars and focusing it. He moved the glasses by millimeters, scanning the road and the underbrush on either side of it. He did not expect to see anything, it was a way of keeping busy. He thought he would have an easier time of it with someone other than Price. Price was a drag on the market, he was all business.

But excellent insurance.

No screwing around with Price, no idle moments. Price was completely professional, the compleat soldier. Still, the nature of the job being what it was, the *irregularity* of it, the volunteer nature of the assignment, Command had asked for reassurances. It was Stringer's play. At Stringer's rates they could not afford a personality clash. The assignment was too delicate.

— Can you work with Price?

— If it's necessary.

— This is no normal patrol, and you're the one with the experience. You two've got to work in harness, and if there's a problem I'd like to know about it now.

— There's no one else?

— No.

— They tell me he's a bloody little martinet.

— But competent.

— We'll stay out of each other's way.

— That's good enough, but you know the way it is.

— I'd rather be in harness with Steinberg.

17

— He's been reassigned.

— Well, I suppose Price it is, then.

— His record is first-class, you'll find him blunt. No light touch, Stringer. Although I don't think, all things considered, that a light touch is what's required.

— So I've heard. But if there's no one else.

— He'll rank you technically. That's one thing the others insisted on. It makes no sense, but there it is.

— But there'll be no shit.

— No, no shit. He understands that.

— Where's Steinberg now?

— Price is strictly professional.

— Steinberg?

— Off duty.

— Here or there?

— Off duty.

And Command had turned away, interview over. In the event, Stringer had worked well with Price. The first day Price hung back, orienting himself, asking questions and deferring his orders. He picked up tricks very quickly, doing it strictly by the book. His memory, Stringer thought, was prodigious. At various points along the way when Stringer told him the book was wrong, Price listened. And appeared to discard the book. Through uncertain territory they moved at a crawl, listening for the smallest sound. More difficult to do than to explain, moving silently, resting at each step. Stringer likened it to the slow stroll of a priest gliding up the aisle of a deserted cathedral. No man for analogy, Price said nothing. But it developed that his language was

18

excellent, almost as fluent as Stringer's. And myomy, how the boy could kill.

At first light they swept the road with the scopes, north and south. They watched for anything with definition, anything moving or shining in the sun. Anything irregular. On his first trip, Stringer had placed a small stick in the middle of the rutted road, figuring that it could be seen through the high-powered scope; but it could not. Still, he was satisfied. It was nothing specific, just a feeling; security. There was nothing human on the road or near it, Stringer was certain of that.

There were two ways to do it, the hard way and the easy way. He could pick his way down the mountainside and through the brush to the point they'd selected. But there was no path that he could see, he'd be obliged to use his machete. That was the hard way, probably eight hours all told. Or he could move down the animal path to the point of the first box, then walk north along the road, moving in and out of brush along the side. That was the easy way and the dangerous way, because he could be readily seen. But the point was to balance six hours against eight, in this instance time was vulnerability. It was wise to gamble, and risk extreme vulnerability for an hour in order to cut the total time by two. That was the basic logic, but Price was adamant in opposition. The easy way was not the logic of the book, far from it.

"Go through the brush, stay the night if you can't get back. Navigation should be very simple, even for a non-navigator."

"No," Stringer said.

"Afraid of a long walk? Man-eating tigers? Poisonous snakes? What's your problem, Stringer?

"I'll watch from here," Stringer said. "If that's the way you want it done, *you* do it. I'll keep tabs. I'll monitor your progress, Price." He knew he was on good ground, Command had been specific on that point. Reconnaissance tactics were his province, although Price was in nominal charge. But Price knew nothing of swift movement, even less about the estimate of danger. And Stringer was wary of Price's instincts.

"Do it the hard way."

"In this case, the hard way's the dangerous way."

"Walking along the road, you expose everything. You put the mission in jeopardy. How the hell do we know that there aren't people in strong points along the road? We don't, Stringer. *We don't know that.* Christ, you'll walk up there like a drum major. And that's that, and the thing's ruined."

"My judgment, Price. I'm taking the walk. I'll decide where to go." He pointed to the road and the points one mile apart. He explained again why it was safest, then strapped on his shoulder holster and prepared to move. Price was silent, standing ramrod straight beside the radio. His big hand rested on the transmitter. "Why don't you make out a report then?" Stringer asked, smiling. "You can build the stockade while I'm gone. Short rations."

Price turned away, expressionless, and Stringer started down the slope, first checking that his weapon was cleaned and loaded and on safety. Cautious Stringer was careful never to carry a loaded gun off safety.

He moved swiftly down the familiar slope, tracking himself. He followed his own trail into the bush, careful to avoid overhanging branches. The branches were alive with red soldier ants, whose bite was like a beesting. The ants fell on his neck and chewed until he killed them with the palm of his hand; insect repellent was useless against the ants. One more irritation. Now that they had made camp, they had to deal with the terrain; when they were marching, they were able to pass it by, enjoy the view, appreciate the land in the abstract. It was not damned pleasant any more, it was huge, barbarous, and unwelcome. The area was said to be inhabited. All the charts and maps so indicated. Aerial reconnaissance so indicated. Ditto intelligence of all varieties. This was an outfit that had more intelligence than it needed, "intelligence" in this case being a hybrid of fact and statistic. Precocious Command supplied the ingenious extrapolations. Truths were nowhere, facts were everywhere; estimates were expressed mathematically. Therefore predictions entered the hard world of numbers. In an area of one hundred square miles, fewer than fifteen "indigenous" people; the computer put it at 13.4 people. Accurate within two percentage points, and Command himself vouched for that; the statistics were verified by high-flying airplanes with the most modern cameras. But the statistics did not disclose the look of the terrain, a brooding dangerous presence, alien, hard, introverted. Stringer could not feel close to it, or part of it, as if it were alive and capable of possession. It would not be possessed, nor did it possess. It was simply *there*, hostile as a person who hates for unexplained reasons. But its dimensions were known to Command, root and branch. He'd made that unmistakably clear at the final briefing. Command took his place before a large illuminated map.

— This is difficult country, you've got to travel minimum light. Damn few rations, not much else. The radio. Weapons. You'll only be there a week, perhaps less, but if we're lucky it'll mean a hell of a lot. You'll have earned it, everything. Reaction time will be less than thirty minutes, we're absolutely at max for this. There's more to it than you know, nothing's being left to chance.

— Weapons?

— Anything you like, that's your option. But you know the score there. You can have them, but if you get your ass in a crack they won't be of much help. More hindrance than help. I'd take a side arm and a hell of a lot of ammunition, but that's me. You do what you like. What you feel most comfortable with. It's no circus.

— Grenades?

— Too bulky, I'd recommend against it. But I don't care. It's your problem. The thing to remember is that this is twenty-four hours. Like the fucking Navy, you ought to go four hours on, four off. If we get the opportunity, we can't let it go by. We'll get only one chance. The sensors should give you plenty of warning. Fitzhugh will brief you thoroughly on those. You'll have plenty of warning time. Don't forget the pills, particularly the halizone, but also the others. A kit's being made up. Rubber poncho, knives, binoculars, scopes, food. That's all being taken care of.

— When we get back . . .

— That information will be available tomorrow morning, just before you leave. Not before.

— O.K.

— You leave tomorrow, we'll have the exact time by 1800 today. You'll know. We'll find you. You'll be briefed on the drop zone and the . . . variables. There'll be a primary and three secondaries. We're not certain which they'll be. That'll be up to you, on the ground. Make your calculations according to the difficulty, estimates of hostility and so forth. It won't do us any goddamned good at all if you're there for two days and then discovered. So be very careful about that. Until 1800, then.

— My time is your time,

Stringer said, and the interview ended.

Now, at first light of the second day on the mountain, he was making his way down the slope to the road. Traveling minimum light, to plant a sensor where it would listen for a convoy. A personal lookout the size and shape of a cigarette pack. The impulse of the sensor would reach them at the mountain's summit, and within minutes — having verified the target — they'd be transmitting to Command. Thirty minutes from transmission to attack, the aircraft summoned by Stringer and Price and guided by other impulses from the sensor (the sensor in this instance doing double duty, the map coordinates fixed to within a dozen meters). The idea was to wait for the convoy to expose itself absolutely then call in the strike, six planes bombing from north to south, right along the road. To obliterate it, a blitz. If they kept their nerve there was virtually no chance of detection. Too many places to hide, too much territory. The enemy had no electronic sensors, no way of knowing for certain where they were. Of course they knew (probably) that there had been a drop, but that was all they knew; they knew where, within a certain perimeter, but he and Price were now fifty miles from the drop zone, and they'd been seen only once, and Price had taken care of that. So they were safe, within reasonable limits. That was the beauty of it, and all that was required now was steadiness, a certain fatalism and nerve.

Stringer reached the road and lay there, waiting. He would wait for twenty minutes, then pick his way north to plant the second box. He hugged the earth, pulling the rough cloth of his black shirt over his wet dark face. He was as close to the earth as it was possible for him to get, listening and watching. He lay in the musky brush, his pistol in his hand, on safety.

Stringer was a loner, on his own, the way he liked it. There was an army behind him, but the army meant nothing now; Price could take care of himself. One way to look at it: he'd implicated no one else. There were no accomplices after the fact. Stringer believed that members of his generation (was it a club, membership conferred by date of birth, the date implying certain other facts: shared history, memories of memories?) were dependent souls, shackled by boredom and protected from the elements. Collapse was just around the corner.

Deadly serious, they had no sense of caprice. They yearned for the control exercised by their fathers. (He'd watched them seeding clouds and had protested mildly to Command: you bastards are screwing around with the *weather;* you're making rain.) Away from it now, farther away than he'd ever been, Stringer despised his own history — the special persistent echo of small American towns, confident families, secure futures. The pitiless joyless advancement along well-worn roads. This spiritual boredom sprung not from decadence or exhaustion, but from fear and suspicion — frightened men turning on narrow compasses. Their success led them away, step by step, from creation. They did not build, they added on; and expired alone and disappointed. Gentler spirits learned to accommodate themselves to the rearranged landscape. *Driven* has a special meaning in the American language.

Or that was the way Stringer looked at it, at night and on assignment, his anger released. Others saw it differently, and with a little effort fitted in; or bent the rules to suit themselves. Stringer was indifferent to rules. He lived within them most of his life, but felt they didn't apply now. When they began to strangle, he simply departed; Stringer was no man for protracted struggle. Lonesome Stringer — he'd departed one family, two schools, one wife, his life at least twice. He thought of himself as something of a paradigm, a success story, his pursuit not of pleasure or security but independence and chaos. A straight line to a vague future, "protected" God knows from what. Money wasn't worth a damn unless independence went with it, the knowledge that he was tied to nothing; no one had a call on him, and he was not afraid. His fees were quite high now, he guessed he was at the top of the line; an independent operator in his own way, except of course that the work was highly specialized. But (and this was the laugh that revealed the fact) he had enough buried in banks to live well and independently for five years or more, until some other thing came along. Habits die hard.

It seemed to him logical to escape to a war, or what was thought to be a war. Perhaps it wasn't a war at all, but a black figment of the imagination. It was not in any case connected to anything else. Different generations escaped the rules in different ways. Most members of his own did not resign but moved on within increasingly vague limits. It was not difficult or dangerous to live in the United States in the 1960s, if you kept your own counsel and avoided conflict and strife. It was an excellent place for a forward observer, someone who was shrewd and sympathetic and in tune, although it was hazardous finding a center of gravity in the muck. It was no good placing value on community, because community was part of the problem and no solution at all. One more petty tyranny, like dangerous drugs, which Stringer had tried and found offensive (fearing an incipient revolt in his head, he viewed drugs as *agents provocateurs* and treated them as he would treat any depraved enemy holding a gun to his temples).

One thing led to another, an excruciatingly logical sequence in one sense, insane in another, and Stringer found himself "attached" to the army, or its civilian counterpart. And why not? As Steinberg explained it, the army was the leading edge of the culture; the army was preparing the battlefield for the various struggles to come. In its mastery of theory and technology (its marriage of virtue and brutality), the army was the institutional da Vinci of the twentieth century. Steinberg explained to the artist, Stringer's ex-wife, that the army could be compared to Kline or Pollock or "any of the other chaps" who'd enlarged man's view of the shape and content of things. Right out there on the edge, Steinberg'd said, and Stringer's wife had stared at him disbelieving; then he told her that it was all a joke, that it contained only a little bit of the truth.

Well. The place where he was bore no relation to any place he had ever known, or ever would know, and he was able to practice his profession (no, it wasn't a profession; it was just something he did well) in the way that prison doctors experimented on inmates. Everyone knew the exact position, there were no mysteries. Not admirable — dreadful, squalid, his friends said. Shameful, wicked. But that was not the point, or not Stringer's point, which was the only point that mattered. If there was a war, it was a citizen's duty to participate in it; Stringer had no taste for self-righteousness. Steinberg defined it as a hunger for complicity. It was now a game without rules, and everyone had to understand what they were up to. No cause for either complaint or alarm, either physical or psychic. No one's civil rights were being violated. Once he'd reached what they were pleased to call his plateau, he was able to choose his assignments. He and Steinberg planned it that way. He chose lonely assignments in the most remote parts of the country. It was his own business, no one else's; he did not see himself as a team player and felt free to refuse their various criminal requests. In that way he was able to fit into the war that they fought. He thought he was reaching a vanishing point in his contact with his former life, a state of mind that suited him; he was an escapee from boredom and security and certainty. And loose rules. A cold star on a fixed orbit, a friend once told him, inevitable and remorseless.

"Just your typical thirty-five-year-old man," he'd told the army doctors.

"Say again?"

"Just your —"

"I don't believe it."

"You'd better."

"In what sense, Mr. Stringer? You tell me, so I can get it straight. For the report we'll write. So that I don't miss anything that I should."

"It's a long story," Stringer said.

"We've got all morning."

"Well, in that case —"

"I've never met anyone like you before. None of us has."

At one turn he was encouraged to believe he was unique (something of a poisonous specimen), and at another a representative member of the representative decade. A vintage year, born at the height of the depression, though it was positively lighthearted compared to the depressions that would come — Class of '35, responsible for nothing, good or bad, in American life. A betweentimes crowd, the backbone of the nation (coming into its own), having managed to evade most of the good and much of the bad of the post-Einstein era, and right now this particular member was as remote as it was possible to be. A man to be envied! A few thousand meters south of Mountain Number 1375, an inaccurate measurement both ways, astride a nameless road. As remote as those in the most secure and progressive asylums in the land, airless, lightless, no life beyond what took place in a few tangled blood cells. A participant in the great adventure, Stringer thought; handsomely rewarded by a proud and grateful nation, anonymous but admired. He was entirely anonymous now, lying belly down in tall grass, listening to fresh sounds. He watched through the interstices of the grass.

An old man, walking a bicycle. Stringer judged him to be sixty or seventy years old, dressed in brown cloth, whistling to himself. He watched the old man's eyes, dull, and his pace, slow. The man's small eyes were trained on the center of the road, he looked to be walking in his sleep. His sandals were nondescript, his bicycle of ancient manufacture. A small bundle was tied to the rear wheel, it looked to be clothing, bobbing like a rabbit's tail. No weapons visible, and Stringer examined the man's body closely, inspecting it for any suspicious marks. Thin as sticks, the old man's legs shuffled along; his ankles were swollen. A few wispy hairs dangled from his chin. Stringer moved the pistol off safety and waited, the possibilities riffling through his mind.

This was an old man who could be what he appeared to be, a traveler. An old farmer going from point A to point B, walking his bicycle, half asleep in the morning sun. Or he could be a scout, inconspicuous, absurdly vulnerable; but knowing that a shot would alert the column behind. Or he could be a courier, carrying a message from one command to another. Stringer, who occasionally had faith in inadvertence, thought that the first was most likely. This old man did not have the strength to walk long distances. His ankles, the look of his chest, the sad eyes, his slow walk. But they would not send a young man to do this job, the young men did other duty; and appearances were always deceptive. The old man was ten yards from him now and he heard the labored breathing — *unh unh unh*. His clothing bore no military markings, and he did not seem alert or curious in any way. The old man looked half asleep. Stringer lay still, his heart pounding against the soft earth, waiting.

Consciously or not, the old man did nothing out of the way. He maintained his pace, his eyes on the road, and Stringer let him go. A calculated risk, and one worth taking. There was no evidence of anything wrong or sinister in any way. Whatever *wrong* was, in these circumstances. Ordinary events were often ominous; the enemy was careful. Stringer exhaled soundlessly, watching the old man and his bicycle lurch out of sight. He allowed another ten minutes to elapse, then stood up. Anyone following the old man would stick closer than ten minutes; but it was strange that anyone was there at all. *That* was definitely out of the ordinary. Thirteen point four inhabitants in a hundred square miles. The road was vacant now, he heard nothing. Stringer was sweating, the beads of cold sweat running down his backbone. He'd been right to let the old man pass, no point whatever in killing or capturing him. Captives made no sense in his situation. There were risks all around, but he was certain he'd done the right thing: he was positive he hadn't been seen, and if that were true it made no difference about the old man. Stringer heaved himself up, quickly crossed to the right side of the road, and flopped down again, buttoned up and still. He waited for another five minutes, saw nothing, and then began to walk north. It was a reasonable imitation of a farmer. Anyone who looked at him from a distance would believe him to be an old party, bent and worn from years in the fields, shoulders bent, arms swinging stiffly; a quiet and purposeful traveler, someone inconspicuous, but moving with deceptive speed.

Price adjusted and focused the scope, but he was unable to tell whether the figure in black was Stringer or someone else. The face was averted. It was probably Stringer, the figure looked to be Stringer's height and weight, but Price couldn't be sure. Stringer had scant aptitude for disguise and was too impatient. Well, if it was Stringer they were doing very well, Price admitted it to himself; that was one *old* man. And if it was someone else, they were in trouble. The result of Stringer's mindless insistence on walking the road instead of the forest.

Command knew the score: *You must assume everything is hostile. Everything that breathes or moves. You can't take a chance. But you must weigh all the consequences. Action, reaction. Cause, effect.*

But Stringer never took the warnings seriously, he

apparently thought he knew more than anybody. More than Command, more than the general staff of the army. But he didn't. He didn't know more than the accumulated experience of the men in Special Action Group, all of whom filed reports and passed on their tricks. Or some of them. As a matter of custom and superstition they did not disclose *all* that they knew, the thing becoming something of a magician's trade after a while. You didn't give away everything any more than Houdini did, and the longer you survived, the more suspicious you became. You withheld some of your findings, thinking they were lucky pieces like a rabbit's foot or a St. Christopher medal or a favorite wristwatch that lost precisely ninety seconds a day.

Stringer — or whoever it was — rounded a bend in the road and was lost to view. Price left the scope and picked up his rifle and reconnoitered the position again. He did this very carefully, as he was taught to do, moving around the perimeter quietly, listening and watching. He wished he had more confidence in Stringer, as he would if Stringer were RA, not a tourist in it for — what? — cash or other valuables. Those people tended to be unstable, to go to pieces when the situation was tight. Stringer was highly recommended, although Command admitted this was his last, or next to last, run. That depended on Stringer himself, his contract expired this month. But Price had heard he'd given hints that he'd extend if the pot were sweetened. No doubt he was valuable, he had more experience than anyone; no doubt he was quick. But he was stubborn, too, and cared nothing for rank. That was all right in its place, but there'd come a time when someone would have to choose. There'd be a tight spot, and someone would have to make a decision for both of them, and when that time came Price knew who would do it. He'd do it if he had to silence Stringer; he'd do it and make it stick. That was what being an army officer was all about. Price was born to lead. Command had told him,

— Listen to Stringer, he knows what he's doing.

Price listened impassively, he was no amateur himself.

— A bit difficult sometimes, not the easiest man to get on with.

— Yes.

— He'll give you no trouble, unless you stumble into one of *his* specialties. Like most of the fellows in SAG, he's a bit spooked. They're a different breed of volunteer, as you know. But that's the way, isn't it?

Stupid civilians, Price thought. In the regular army when a man was spooked he was relieved. All of the symptoms were obvious, and there was a procedure for removal. Then you reached down into the manpower pool and pulled out another number. The regular army was a pool of interchangeable parts, and that was its virtue. These others, they scarcely knew what they had in reserve. They were elitist, and that was not the military way. If something worked they kept it going until it fell apart or failed in some other way. *They did not plan.* In the RA they knew better. They had ways of telling.

Price leaned against a rock and relieved himself. He would've gone down there with the box himself, but that was against the general order. He was to operate the radio (repair it if necessary) and keep the code. Stringer was not to know the code, if anything happened to Price all transmissions would be *en clair*. A stupid procedure, but there it was. Price was not to leave the laager, except in extraordinary circumstances; that was contraindicated, Command said. Christ, the civilians. They fucked up everything they touched, they had no sense of order or discipline. No understanding of obedience. No sense of method. Price considered. Useful facts.

Mustard gas smells like garlic.
Lewisite like geraniums.
Tear gas like flypaper.
White phosphorus like matches.
Phosgene like new-mown hay.
Thermit like nothing.

These were important facts, well to have in hand. No one had used mustard gas in more than forty years, but they would sometime soon. And when they did, Price would be able to identify it and take the proper precautions. Mustard gas produced boils the size of eggs on arms, legs, backs. Terribly painful, the doctors said, and difficult to heal. After the first few days the eggs broke and the arm or leg looked like it had taken a third-degree burn, which in a way it had. You dealt with this by preparing yourself mentally. Winter was the most dangerous period, the effects could linger for weeks. Phosgene was no sweat, coughing for a few hours; an irritation of the lower lung. Lewisite: body poisoning (!).

Doubtless there were other gases that he knew nothing about, as there were numerous weapons and advanced

34

tactics. Command did not share all that it knew. Some facts and situations were withheld from the men in the line. There was good and sufficient reason for this.

Price scanned the road again with his binoculars, snapping them smartly into place when he detected movement. Price stood tall, flexed his muscles, and waited. He saw a figure dart across the road and disappear into the bush. That would be Stringer, he'd moved a quarter of a mile since the last sighting. Price kept his glasses on the spot at the side of the road, watching with great care. Presently he saw a bent man rise and go shuffling off down the road. A decent imitation, Price thought. For Stringer, not bad. Price watched him move down the road fifty yards, then round another curve and disappear from sight. His field of vision was bare again. Nothing stirred.

It would take him longer than they'd calculated.

two

LONG BEFORE the war, Stringer and his wife lived in New Hampshire and took long walks at night. Six, eight miles — they'd walk until midnight or two in the morning, in delight to pause and make love beside the road. He always carried a small blanket or wore a coat they could use to lie on. Evenings in New Hampshire were chilly, even in mid-July. They walked close together, bumping shoulders, talking in whispers. The walks were the best part of the day, the work done and done well, he'd tell himself, and the walk at night a reward for hard labor. He was studying history then. That was when he was first married, and finishing up at a small college. They had a cabin near the top of a mountain and he'd go to class half the day and read the other half and walk at night with his wife. They existed in a physical intimacy and understood each other very well in the beginning.

This was a deserted mountain road, and they seldom encountered anyone else. If a car approached late at night, they'd consider their privacy violated. Their road, they said; their darkness. Stringer's wife was a shy self-possessed woman who lived with her dream of becoming an artist, and this in the face of demands that she prepare a home. Stringer was no man to withhold complaints. When she broke down and cried, this would silence him for a day or two. He didn't want to hurt her, only make her understand that they had to fortify each other. Life was difficult and sometimes dangerous, and it was often necessary to prepare barricades. He didn't know what would happen after New Hampshire, perhaps nothing would. Really, he wanted to bend her to his will.

When the marriage collapsed it simply fell apart, all the strings broken. They had no double knots (her phrase) to hold them together. Later he thought of their marriage as symptomatic of the times, fragile and fatalistic, withdrawn; they were not determined people. When everything collapsed, friends and family rallied round to try to put it together again. But there wasn't anything left, just some old attitudes and memories. They'd not fortified each other. They'd never settled or made any life together, and Stringer was forced to wonder what it was that they had and what they lost. In the beginning they had loved each other and were attached in a physical way. For better or worse he remembered the New Hampshire period as a good one, particularly the long walks in the evening, dark trees soaring overhead, the stars laid out against the sky in mysterious constellations, a crisp breeze; pine needles, the smell of the earth, dark pockets, small animals scuttling away at their approach.

He tried to remember what they talked about. It seemed to him they talked about each other, but it was nearly fifteen years ago now, and difficult for him to summon memory from that distance. They talked about what he'd do, he thought for a time that he'd be a newspaper reporter. It would be interesting and valuable to be at the center of events, watching things unfold. He did not have the patience for history, and he thought of his own life as a current event. Wouldn't it be an experience to be in on the inside, to inspect the mechanism? She was reserved, but mostly favorable; she thought it sounded exciting. She would paint in her atelier, and he would bring the world to her; he would be her Oxford and her Cambridge. Journalism sounded glamorous and vaguely racy, a voyeur's dream or nightmare. He thought it was a way to position himself just outside the line of fire, to be in it but not of it; a respectable compromise. At various times he'd meant to be a newspaper reporter, a pilot, an architect, a soldier, a musician.

He supposed that they talked of momentary things, the way their lives moved together; what was hazardous and what was not. They were too young to think seriously of the future, but it was always with them, a coming attraction. Things were seen in the light of the future and the available possibilities. When the time came to consider a newspaper job he accepted the first offer without discussing the matter with her. He wanted it to be a surprise. The newspaper was in Chicago, and he remembered the town from his year at the university; the year with Steinberg and Boone and the others. He remembered its look and smell, and he liked what he remembered. But in the event, the job turned into something quite different from what he expected. He extracted facts from documents and arranged them into stories. "Winnowing" they called it. In the beginning it was interesting work, but later on it became tedious and unsettling. After a year on the job Stringer was fired during one of the paper's periodic economy waves. He was fired, and happy. He desired something real.

She pushed out on her own and went to school, nine to twelve, days, at the Art Institute. Stringer read books in their apartment in Hyde Park and occasionally sought work. He couldn't connect with what he saw around him. He read a novel by Thomas Hardy and resolved to find employment as a lapidary, figuring that carving gravestones would supply him with a purchase on the future. But there were machines to do that now, and apprenticeships were demanding. In Chicago there was the possibility of becoming a professional thief (or the next best thing, a police sergeant) — he talked this over with friends at the Compass, a long inquiry into the social utility of the outlaw. He got as far as casing one joint. Drawing plans, routes of access, getaways, hideouts. But in the end it was only a long laugh (a month's laugh, in fact) and he went back to his books. He undertook a review of the century's war novels, puzzled by the latent exhilaration in them. Novelists were hypnotized by danger, and how it was shared and met; persistence in the face of violence and death.

His wife, baffled, kept her distance. Toward the end of the period in Chicago, Stringer turned to darker novelists and argued — in the evening, his long day over, propped up in a morris chair beside the window — that the common experience of mankind was murder in its various forms. To Stringer that explained a good deal, although the country was temporarily at peace. There were no wars in sight. His wife was the one in touch, painting seriously now, preparing for a show; her subject was the miraculous lakefront, waves and beaches and happy citizens sunning themselves in the sand. Life as a long and succulent Boating Party, he told her. Keep at it, a winning metaphor.

She looked at him helplessly.

— What one reads has very little to do with what one sees. Perhaps there's a war on without our knowing it.

— We'd know it.

— A mysterious war.

— What is it with you and the war?

— Your Boating Party, my war.

He watched her improve month by month, she was especially appealing at her easel. Poised, it seemed her feet never touched the ground as she stood before the painting, one hand with her brush, the other massaging the small of her back. One August she did not attend classes at the Art Institute and they went to ground together in the small apartment in Hyde Park. It was the hottest summer in the history of the city, and some days they'd spend the morning and afternoon in bed, a dime-store fan blowing on a pitcher of ice water. In the evenings they'd leave the apartment for a movie or for the grass on the Midway, to lie on their backs and stare at the stars. It was in some ways an agreeable summer, she was planning her first show and he had discovered the literature of the First World War. The portable television set always waited for them in the bedroom, a dog-eared *TV Guide* beside it — "My Oxford and my Cambridge," she called it.

Returning from a day's trip downstate at the height of the heat wave, he proposed that they leave Chicago. They needed a clean slate, the heat was sucking them dry, the atmosphere of the city was suffocating. It was a concrete wasteland, and Hyde Park was no longer safe — it was often infiltrated now by marauding gangs. The character of the university was subtly changing. Their apartment was a prison, and he could see no future in the city.

This had been a very bad and depressing day downstate, visiting a friend who'd tried suicide. Stringer's wife was appalled by the state hospital and frightened by the friend.

"This place has become oppressive," he said. "And I'm tired . . . of looking *on*."

Distracted, she nodded in agreement.

"Perhaps the West," he said.

"Why not the East?"

"West is new, East is old."

She shook her head. It made no sense. The city seemed strange to her, and Stringer was more remote than ever. He'd retreated. Was she tied to him forever?

Discouraged, he felt that time was running out, possibilities dwindling. What had happened to the future? "I'm open to any suggestions," he said.

"Wasn't it awful, there." She meant the state hospital. "Wasn't it fearful. I hated it. God, the guards. The *orderlies*. Bars on the windows. The muttering. The smell. The gray buildings. I can't believe that there wasn't any warning with him, that it happened like turning off a light. I can't believe there weren't indications, signals of some kind. Looking at him, you know very well he isn't going to get better. You know it. It's a look he has."

They were driving in the outskirts of Chicago, and the city's heat began to close in on them. The dirt was real and visible, the heat turned the asphalt into a mirage. Old people sat on the front stoops of brownstones, fanning themselves and talking aimlessly. In this part of the city the stoplights were not synchronized. Stop start, stop start. They sat in the car, waiting for the green, sweating.

"He might get better," Stringer said. It depressed and angered him to think of his friend forever locked up. "Drugs, one thing and another. Some *do* improve. It's not hopeless."

She was silent, her face turned away from him, staring out the window. She remembered the man's face, lean and ill-shaven, and the eyes, unnaturally bright.

"Well, at least we're all right," he said.

She looked at him blankly.

"We're together anyway."

"Well, we're not in there. Yet. If that's what you mean. I don't know exactly what you have in mind by 'all right.' That's a bit vague for me, I don't get it." She was stunned by what she thought was his callousness, his refusal to face obvious facts. He hated facts, he lived in an unreal world. A world of one, she thought.

"What do you think about the West?" he said after a minute.

"Sure," she said, agreeing automatically. Her habit over many years. "Anywhere, just so I can buy paints."

"Denver, L.A."

"Denver."

"You could paint up a storm in Denver."

"And exactly what do you intend to do?" she was staring straight ahead, at the Cottage Grove mirage. "Just so I'll know. What'll be your field in Denver, Colorado."

He shrugged, eyes on the stoplight.

"Yes?"

"This and that."

"Once," she said angrily. "Just *once* . . ."

"Not looking *on*," he said with a smile. "Not to end . . ."

"Yes yes yes yes yes of course yes," she said.

The summer ended and the heat disappeared, and a long silence began. There were no more movies or late-night walks to the Midway, and no references to "there." They watched their box in desperation. The crisis passed, the knots unraveled, and she returned to her painting and he to his books. There was no energy left. He proposed a trip to New Hampshire, where they'd last connected with each other. The West was out of the question now, it seemed too difficult and hazardous; the details were overwhelming. But she refused to return East: that was part of the past, and there was no going back to it.

44

Steinberg's call decided everything. Steinberg, missing for a year, called him at home late one night. Stringer's wife answered the telephone and recognized the voice (he'd called twice before over the years, always late at night, always with disruptive results). She listened to him for a minute, then handed the receiver to her husband without comment. She turned over, her face to the wall, and listened to their nonsense, their private language. Steinberg and Stringer reminisced together about their early days at the university: the Compass players, the demise of Boone, the long hours laughing over beer in darkened bars. None of this had anything to do with her, she came later. After ten minutes the laughing stopped, and the conversation turned serious. Stringer lit his second cigarette. She listened to his voice with tears in her eyes.

— You're kidding me, Steinberg.

. . . .

— How did it happen?

. . . .

— I don't believe it. It's hard to believe. I'll give you credit, Steinberg. It's your greatest act.

. . . .

— I'd never thought of you in that line of work, old friend. I had not thought of you at freedom's first line of defense. I saw you as more or less a *free* . . . agent.

. . . .

— I'm at loose ends, ready for anything. To answer your question, the newspaper washed out.

. . . .

— Bored, Steinberg! Bored!

45

. . . .

—Wait till I get a pencil. You're incredible.

And a week after that, Stringer was on a plane to Washington. The interviews were tedious but successful, the authorities did not seem to care about his failure with journalism. He proceeded from one tiny cubicle to another, questioned by kindly tweedy men in horn-rimmed glasses. The tests were entirely psychological and Steinberg had briefed him well (they'd sat in a room in the Mayflower Hotel until well after midnight, Steinberg talking and Stringer listening: *commitment*, Steinberg repeated again and again in his precise monotone). In three days, Stringer returned to Chicago as a provisional employee of the American government. They celebrated with a steak dinner at the Buttery. Three hours of cocktails and wine, and Stringer talked nonstop; they were off dead center at last, they'd live well. The period of irresponsibility was over. Washington was pleasant, a change of scene. He had a worthwhile job and was committed to it, and she could continue her painting . . .

She shook her head. She did not want to leave the Art Institute.

"What difference does it make where you paint? Here or there?"

"It makes a difference to me."

"Well?"

"I did it first here. The classes, my show."

"But . . ."

"Can't you understand that?"

"Yes," he said with relief.

All this, so dry. The facts of his life, incompletely recalled. He'd forgotten the essence of their love, the things that drew them together. He remembered only sentimental things, her smile, the way her hair fell, her breasts up close, her wit. The one hot summer in the city, and the way they'd survived it. He thought now that love had served him badly, he'd deserved better. So had she. But he remembered with fondness the late-night walks in New Hampshire, and the loony mornings in Chicago, and the innocence of history books.

Where he was now, the heat and humidity flattened things and made them soft; the terrain was featureless. People exulted: what a beautiful country! What a shame. Isn't it gorgeous! Too bad. But it wasn't a beautiful country at all, it was too green, too damp; things had the look of death. The hills that rose on either side of him were snub-nosed, and thick with vegetation. They were low and suffocating, their contours resembled men at sleep.

He swung off the road and moved silently into the brush and lay still. A cigarette pack touched his nose, it had no odor of tobacco. He yearned for a cigarette, for anything that would relieve the tension. He lay still for five minutes, then raised himself and continued walking north, toward the objective. At this rate of speed he'd need two hours more. He looked at the mountain looming over him, but saw nothing out of the ordinary. The mountain's slopes looked as flat and hard as concrete. He imagined Price cursing, following his progress through the telescope. Around him, silence. Away off in the bush he heard a vague rustle of leaves and reflected again how sad it was that there were no birds in that part of the country.

They maintained radio silence, although the chance for detection was almost nil. Every ninety minutes they were supposed to open the key to receive urgent messages, if any; there were strict rules governing SOS signals. Command knew where they were and if something happened — well, there were assumptions that would be made. Price looked at the radio with distaste, it was one of the new light models. It looked like a piece of Swedish furniture, a modish Scandinavian blend of wood and metal. More powerful, tougher, more efficient, more complex, more expensive than the conventional issue. Old Reliable was another casualty of war and technology. Old Reliable that a child could operate and repair. This new machine was a wonder.

Price did not understand it as he understood the RA model, which was simple and built along classical lines. This new one, intricate as a Swiss watch, required a trained radio technician. They'd sent Price to radio school for six weeks, and those were mind-numbing weeks. He'd told them that he was a soldier not a . . . *repairman*. Even after six weeks of training, his understanding of the radio was imperfect.

Price moved to the edge and looked down. The road was empty, Stringer was nowhere to be seen. He disliked solitude, preferring the security of numbers. He was an infantry officer, not a scout. Miscast, Price thought. He was miscast as a guerilla and as a radioman. He was happiest when surrounded by people and things, symbols of his country and his profession. This place where he was; it was too isolated — and would be frightening except for its beauty. It was the most beautiful country Price had ever seen.

He worked back from the edge and raised the radio antennae. Then he set the dial and threw the switch to receive incoming messages. These were not to be acknowledged, unless acknowledgment was specifically requested.

He listened to static for a moment. Then, "Dance One this is Dance Two."

Price jumped for his notebook and pencil, lying atop the radio set.

"Dance One this is Dance Two. Acknowledge."

"Dance One acknowledges. Eleven-fifty-four."

"Dance One message commences:

| 65733 | 89045 | 35634 | 11309 | 58345 | 80990 |
| 47037 | 86572 | 65294 | 15467 | 22801 | 00294 |

Message ends."

"Dance One acknowledges."

The radio fell silent.

It was a simple five-figure code, the last number in each group indicating the number to be eliminated. (When the numeral was more than five, the entire group was eliminated.) Price dug into his pocket for the decoder, an ingenious scrap of paper that could be taken for anything — doodles, a laundry list, weapons designations. But in the event of capture, it was the first item swallowed. Price was surprised, Command was not to transmit except in an emergency. Perhaps they were disappointed at no action, although he and Stringer had been on the lookout less than two days. It had taken them a day longer than anticipated to arrive, but that was unimportant. Price bent over the radio set, decoding the message, which read: *Urgent you remain additional week.*

He was dismayed, they had neither food nor water for ten days. Stretching the supply, they could endure one week; they'd found no water en route. Water was necessary, unlike food (this was not the ordinary patrol, with hot meals and frosty cans of beer at the end of the march). The heat pounded on the mountain and sucked moisture from a man's body, the humidity acted as a sponge. They're insane, Price thought. Insane civilians who hadn't thought out the order. They had less than a quarter of a canteen of water a day, and that was not nearly enough. He stood with the message in his hand, then put a match to it.

Obviously, Command expected a big move and was apprehensive about sending a relief. There was no one else to send, anyway; Stringer was the last of the professionals. The others were either casualties or retired or otherwise unavailable. Steinberg, Stringer's regular partner, was said to be in another part of the country. So they would have to stick and make the best of it. But this was a typical civilian foul-up, a foul ball, one more indication of a chronic sickness. They did not understand about proper support. It had to do with the theory of command and control, and proper backup. In the military, there were agreed procedures. Unless A and B were in place, C could not happen. That was obvious, they'd explained it all to him at Culver and at the Point and at

Benning and Bragg and the other places. His colonel father explained it to him. It was in all the books, a commandment. In the military, every man had his job to do and you did not send men out beyond their limits. You demanded one hundred percent performance within the agreed limits, but you did not demand one hundred and ten percent because there was no such thing. One hundred and ten percent did not exist, except in the minds of amateurs.

Goddamned amateurs, Price thought. Stringer's people.

He picked up the binoculars and swung them over the terrain. Certainly there were streams somewhere, but none were visible; the land lay under a green blanket. It would be dangerous as hell to move off the mountain again (you only took such risks as guaranteed a reasonable chance of success, and those could be beautifully calculated). There would surely be patrols in advance of the convoy. If there was a convoy. If the whole thing were not another wild goose chase. Although possibly not, it depended on what *they* had available. Where were their Steinbergs? How threatened did they feel, did they operate on hunch? And those facts were impossible to know, although estimates were available. There were estimates on everything, broken down into fractions. Price wished he had an estimate just then, a military estimate assembled by a shrewd and clever G-2, someone who had access to all the numbers and a good head to add them up. But estimate or no, they *would* be obliged to go off the mountain in search of water. That much was certain. There could be no air drop, for the same reason that they had not been ferried all the way by helicopter; the chances of detection were too great. Well, if they could find the water the halizone would purify it. Undrinkable potable water, which was better by far than no water at all.

Civilians. They lived by different rules.

He could see no streams through the glasses, although he knew they were there. The map showed him that, although the map was largely inaccurate; the positioning of streams and rivers might be as much as five miles off. The map was no real help, but it could be a guide; a hint to a rumor. Price hoped that Stringer was wise enough to fill up his own canteen if he found any water. Price worried the problem for a moment, then put it out of his mind. A practical man, no romantic, his life had been spent at army bases, a symmetrical world of barracks and officers' rows, taps and reveille, rectangular formations, and relentless military language. An orderly world, neat as a pin and well starched; punctual, scrupulous. Actions that had consequences, causes that had effects. Nothing random, and very little wild. Price observed doubt as a man coming indoors from the bright light of a sunny day. Blinded, he was both truculent and frightened.

But now as he scanned the valley through the glasses, he knew he must formulate a plan. Something simple and direct, a straight line between two points. He thought that he'd never seen a land so beautiful; how tragic that it should be scarred by war, how sad. Simple people caught in lethal cross fire, no escape available to them. The Middle Ages were the best war years, when armies fought each other and civilians stayed clear. He liked the land. The virgin hills with their soft edges, rolling west, growing bigger and taller; fifty miles west the massif began, a nearly impenetrable and unexplored mountain chain. A fabulous forest. The land was set in various shades of green, black-green in the pockets and light where the sun's rays hit it. Here and there an individual tree thrust higher than the rest, spoiling the harmony. A good place to hide. But the effect was smooth and regular, a mountain paradise innocent of civilization.

It was time to beat into the bush again, and Stringer slipped off the road and flopped down. The road was barely wider than a towpath now, the vegetation grew so quickly. It'd probably been a month or more since any heavy traffic had passed, although the ruts were there and obviously fresh. He had thirty minutes more, no longer than that. He felt inside his shirt for the sensor and held it for a moment. Very conscious now of his hearing, he listened with effort, straining forward, his hand curled around his ear. There was no breeze and the heat hung in heavy breaths. He looked at his watch, noon. Then he unhooked the flat canteen and took a small swallow of water; it held only twelve ounces, perfectly concealed under his clothing. He knew he'd be dead tired when he returned that night and considered for the first time taking the easy way back. It was easy but infinitely more dangerous. Having planted the box, the objective achieved, the idea was to get into the bush as quickly as possible. He lay in hiding for another five minutes, then heaved himself up and resumed his awkward march down the rutted road.

Stringer calculated his position after an hour of walking and reckoned that he had only fifteen minutes to go. His legs were hurting some, but he was not tired. In an hour's time, the character of the road had subtly changed. There was more junk on the shoulders, odd bits of metal, pieces of paper, an occasional broken water flask. He could see where the road had been repaired, bomb craters filled in, the grade smoothed. He was moving very slowly, sweeping the road with his eyes. He was spooked, it was too quiet. Nervous without knowing why, he angled off the road again and nestled into the bush, hiding himself well. When next he'd move he'd go all the way, plant the box and get out without delay. He was operating on the odds now, having walked twenty minutes and seen nothing, he would hide himself for ten or fifteen. He'd decided to return the hard way, through the forest on the slope of the mountain. He thought the road was unlucky, that there was too much character to it, too much evidence of use.

Yes, and yes again.

Caution rewarded.

Stringer smiled to himself and made a silent bow of congratulations when he heard the voices. He was backed up against a small bush, completely hidden. He'd taken unusual care, since this was the last time he'd have to do it. The road was fifteen yards in front of him, he had a full view through the brush and unless the intruders had eagles' eyes he was safe. Branches fell over his head, and he peeped through them. He had all the view he needed, and room to maneuver the pistol from its shoulder holster to his hand and then to his eyes, where he had a clear shot.

They toddled into view, two old men. They were more

than old, they were ancient, or seemed so, all bone and flesh and slack tendons. Their dark skin shone like old leather. Stringer made the same checks he did with the first old one, noting clothes and shoes and bundles. These two carried a single bundle apiece, slung over their shoulders in the manner of an American hobo. They walked very slowly and smoothly, careful where they put their feet; that part was not feigned, he was certain of that. He worked out the odds in his mind and they were astronomical. There were no people in that part of the country, or so the statistics said, and in this instance the statistics were doubtless accurate. First one old man, now two. There was no reason to walk down this road, it was an army supply road. Not a road to market or to anywhere else a civilian would be thought likely to go. In the circumstances it was not plausible. He remembered Command's stilted language. *Not within the parameters,* Command liked to say.

The two halted in the middle of the road, and one of them shuffled to the far side to relieve himself. Stringer thought he looked like Charlie Chaplin with his splayed feet and tattered black clothing and look of sullen innocence. All he lacked was a cane, a derby hat, and a moustache. The other had something of the melancholy manner of Stan Laurel, a long bony face, high cheekbones, and clumsy walk. His eyes were at half-mast. They were some pair, he thought. Some pair of men to find on a deserted road in a deserted part of the country, in advance of a military convoy. Stan Laurel and Charlie Chaplin as the advance scouts of an army: entirely plausible.

There was one more irregularity. This road ran — how long? Twenty miles, a hundred and twenty miles? Wasn't it a coincidence that Chaplin decided to take a leak where Stringer could see him. All the places there were to leak, all the hundreds and thousands of trees and bushes and places by the side of the road to amble over and piss. But he had not chosen any of those, he had chosen the place directly in front of Stringer; in his sights, in fact. His backbone a perfect bull's eye. While the other, Laurel, stood in the center of the road and scuffed his foot, moving it back and forth, leaving a channel approximately the size and depth of the Erie Canal. Neither of them had looked in his direction, and it seemed to him now that they had looked everywhere else, to the left and right, backward and forward, up and down. But that could be simple paranoia. Stringer told himself again never to discount simple paranoia.

Chaplin emerged again, scratching himself, and the two of them squatted down. Laurel produced a flask from his bundle and something edible and they both began to eat and drink, chattering all the while. Laurel divided the food slowly and with care, as if measuring the grams. Chaplin watched him indulgently, his face breaking into a slight smile. They were speaking very softly, so Stringer could not catch all of it. Chaplin appeared to be talking about one of his sons, who was serving the fatherland in the army, or preparing to serve the fatherland, and his mother was fretting, worried about his safety. Laurel was doing the listening, and when he interjected it was to complain about women. The two of them were otherworldly comical, squatting in the middle of the road, gesturing and sliding off each other with words. The language was so difficult and imprecise, it was a language of hints and rumors of hints, heavenly in metaphor and soft in line. Stringer listened with effort, he thought he was getting about every third word. Then he gave it up, he had to concentrate on other things.

Too much coincidence.

In a random world, these two old men were outside the norm. Any norm, however it was defined. Stringer had stayed alive for twelve months by obeying percentages, and now he saw terrible violations. So he was lying with his pistol in his hand, trying to figure the best and most efficient and safest method of getting rid of the two old men without arousing suspicion (what to do with them?) and if possible without killing them. Whether or not they were working for an army just then, they were certainly farmers by trade; Stringer knew that by the look of their hands, hard and bony and partly withered. No fingernails. They were two comical old men: Laurel kept his hands clasped in front of him rocking back and forth on his heels, eating and drinking with deliberation and great pleasure. Stringer's fist tightened on the butt of the gun. He saw no way to avoid it. Sweat streamed down his forehead and into his eyes, he was looking away from the two old men, checking the road again. There was no one else, or no one he could see. His stomach muscles tightened, and he could feel the nerves in his body, a gentle trembling; the surface of his skin was electric to the touch. He wished to hell this hadn't happened, that he'd been twenty minutes faster or they'd been twenty minutes slower. It was bad luck and bad coincidence all around.

They were playing it right up to the line, sitting and waiting for the main element. That had to be it, there was no other explanation. It took plenty of courage to do that, knowing (as they must know) that an armed man, an enemy, was off the trail. They were waiting for their comrades and daring him to take the main chance.

Stringer was worried about the noise, although he could do it in two shots. The knife was dangerous because he may have misjudged his men; they might be armed, and younger and tougher than they seemed. But if they were the advance party — Chaplin and Laurel, incongruous point men — it meant that another group of some kind was behind them, probably quite close. He couldn't imagine how they spotted him, unless there were outposts along the road, in which case he'd be dead now. No, that was not possible. But coincidence had built up and was impossible to ignore. He would be a fool to ignore it, although silencing — killing — these men contained risks as well. He'd been obliged to do it only twice before, and both times the men had been uniformed soldiers; he had not minded killing soldiers at close range, where the rules were clear. Just now the rules were a little less clear.

He heard one of them say that it was time to go.

The other nodded, neither agreement nor disagreement.

Another five miles to travel.

That, or something close to it. Five miles or three hours, conceivably two if there was no interference.

58

If they walked with speed.

If the weather held.

And they were not interrupted.

The two old men stood and dusted themselves off. They took a minute to adjust their bundles and clean them of stray bits of dirt. All of this was very slow and deliberate. Laurel replaced his water flask and his food. They stood for a moment in the center of the road, smiling at each other and nodding. Chaplin's expression was somewhere between a smile and a sneer; Stringer disliked his face, it moved in quick darting gestures. But possibly that was a reaction to the situation, they were now under heavy pressure. Their words and gestures were formal. Stringer thought that Chaplin was thanking Laurel for the food and drink, but they were speaking so softly that it was difficult for him to tell. They walked off then, their pace quickening. Revived by food, the two old men walked off side by side, swaying a little, their bundles slung, the rough sandals scraping the path. They were arm in arm, and their shoulders touched as they walked; Laurel was bent toward Chaplin, the two old men were supporting each other. Stringer heard their voices recede, then he looked back the way they had come. The road was empty as far as he could see it, vacant of any living thing. He listened, his ear to the ground and then in the air. He lay absolutely still, his nerves fluttering. There were no rules for it, Stringer was running on instinct alone. It was not quite murder. It was something short of that. But when they'd advanced about twenty yards, he lifted his pistol, aimed carefully, and fired twice. He put a single shot into one, then the other. He took Chaplin first, on the outside, then Laurel. The shots were good and both men, torn from each other, pitched forward and fell brokenly, and lay still.

The shots boomed like cannon, and Stringer waited a moment before venturing into the road. He was deafened by the reports, and momentarily confused by what he'd done. He hurried out of the bush and searched both men and then dragged them off the road. He pulled Laurel off the road first, then went back for Chaplin; they were light as feathers. He felt Chaplin twitch and heard him mutter something. It sounded like an apology or curse of some kind, but he looked at Stringer with blank eyes. Stringer let go of Chaplin and wiped his hands on the old man's tunic. Blood stained the road, bright red, unmistakable: they both had gaping wounds in their backs. He dug a shallow grave very hastily, plunging his knife into the soft earth, scraping a trench. Chaplin's breath rattled, and then he commenced to moan. Stringer listened to him while he labored over the shallow grave. The moan became a high whine. He administered a coup de grace by suffocation. He was glad it was Chaplin and not Laurel. He reckoned he'd been wise to kill them both, Chaplin was wearing an expensive wristwatch and Laurel was carrying an army compass. Wristwatches and compasses belonged to a different world, and that was the decisive play. But in every other respect, the two old men appeared to be simple farmers.

three

_____

". . . NOTHING ON either one of them, no papers, no military gear of any kind. Just the watch and the compass, souvenirs now. I buried them as best I could, then got the hell out of there. The box is secure. I saw no one else. You better write that down, Price. Or commit it to memory. They'll want a report. They'll want yours as well as mine. They'll want to know."

"How deep?"

"Not very, I had no shovel. Or entrenching tool, as you people call it. And I wasn't anxious to do a Forest Lawn, Price. I used my knife, and the earth was soft. They're just barely below the surface."

"They'll stink."

"That's right. To the sky."

"How far off the trail?"

"I took them maybe twenty, thirty yards in. The underbrush becomes quite thick. They couldn't've weighed over a hundred pounds apiece, bag of bones, both of them. Two old farmers finking for the army. Nothing more."

"Why did you kill them, Stringer?"

"I told you that. It went against the odds. I couldn't take chances, I thought they were marking the spot. Too much coincidence, and I've learned to distrust that. If you stick with this business, Price, you'll learn to distrust it, too. There isn't anything else to go on but beautiful instinct, and you'll learn to obey it. Too fucking much coincidence."

"I look at it the opposite way. If they'd been scouting and seen or suspected you, they never would have stopped to eat right where you were. That was very stupid, no scout would do that. They would have kept on going, marked the spot in some way. What the Christ percentage is it to put yourself in somebody's sights? Why —"

"Well, they're dead now."

"Yes, but —"

"We'll never know, will we? It'll be our little mystery, Price. Yours and mine."

They argued for an hour, until finally Stringer told Price to shut up. Price was some lulu, he should have known right away; one look at Price's dossier revealed the man, a military temperament. And insecure in areas outside his own competence, figuring the inspector general hid behind every tree and rock. And Price would get worse before he got better, there was no doubt of that; he was a man with a single track, with no margin for confusion. Still, Stringer felt bad about the two old men, he'd watched them for fifteen minutes and felt now that he knew them. One had a son due to fight for the fatherland, the other had a nagging wife. Doubtless there were daughters as well, and the old men were probably grandfathers. Chaplin got his face from living in his godforsaken country, it was a place that could make a man very mean. God knows where they were headed; hell, they were probably headed *home*. With a compass? A wristwatch? A farmer didn't need a compass to direct him from one village to another, nor did he need a Japanese wristwatch with a sweep second hand and a date on its face. But to the naked eye they were just two old duffers walking home, arm in arm, talking about their families, stopping for a bite of food and drink in the center of a road, in the middle of nowhere. Nowhere to him, somewhere to them. Chaplin and Laurel. Stringer reflected for a moment that they were entirely foreign references; the two old men had no appreciation of film comedians. Probably they had never seen a film. Or, conceivably, fired a weapon. They sat quietly and ate and enjoyed each other. And fifteen minutes later lay dead, their lives ended in explosions. What a hell of a waste. But they had the bad luck to do the wrong things in the wrong sequence. The sequence of events couldn't be ignored.

Bad odds, Stringer thought.

Wrong time, wrong place.

And why would a farmer carry a compass?

Well, he would not win the Albert Schweitzer Award

this month. That would go to warmhearted Price, the farmer's friend. He'd personally nominate Price. The awards were made whenever their group thought to make them, usually late at night around the bar of the O Club. The winner was bought drinks and presented with a white feather. Price's story was the sweetest story of the year, no question of that. Warmhearted pragmatic Price.

He lay with his shoulders against the big rock, the paperback opened in his lap. He took responsibility for his actions, although he knew they were the product of training as much as of character; he obeyed the law of survival in pursuit of an objective. In that way he was forced to do what he did, and the eventual correctness of an action — whether or not it "worked" — was of no account. It was like asking whether a thunderstorm "worked." The thunderstorm, like Stringer's life, simply *was*.

"Shit," he muttered.

"What?"

"Nothing."

"What did you say, Stringer?"

"I said I'm going to take a piss," Stringer said, heaving himself to his feet. He walked thirty yards away and peered over the edge of the rock to the valley and the road and the river beyond it. He reconnoitered, looking again for any signs of enemy. There were none. Nothing on top, nothing below. No movement anywhere.

"I'm thinking about the water, Stringer."

The war with Price was getting on his nerves, Stringer thought it was just as well to bend a little. Price was a pain in the ass, but he was all there was. He was young, he'd learn. They'd be together for a week, and there was no avoiding that. If they stayed alive, they'd stay together, and they needed each other. Their isolation was complete and would get worse. He could get along with Price as a fellow professional. "What do you think?"

"I think one of us ought to go look for water. If they want us to stay an extra week, we'll need it."

An improvement.

"Four canteens isn't enough. There's no way to spread it to make it last. No way." Price looked at him.

"It's a lot less than half a canteen a day, the only man I know who can get along on that is Steinberg."

"Too bad Steinberg isn't here, then."

"No it isn't," Stringer said.

"This ever happen to you before?"

Stringer shook his head, it never had. He'd never been out for more than a week at a time, a week was supposed to be the maximum run. Water had never been a problem. There were other problems, ammunition, illness, bad weather, fear, technical foul-ups. But never water.

"You didn't see any near the road?"

"Nothing," Stringer said. "No streams, no standing water. I didn't take the old duffers' water because I figured we didn't need it, and I like traveling light. There's the big river, but that's fifteen miles away." He considered. "Maybe twenty. And you've got to cross the road to get to it, and then come back. That's too *damn* risky, and there are people over there." Stringer waited for the response to that, but Price was silent.

Well, there's got to be a stream around here someplace. Or a pond or something." Stringer looked at Price.

"I'll go," he said finally.

A definite improvement.

"I appreciate the suggestion, but I probably better."

"What the hell," Price said. "You've done it. You've made two trips already. I'll go down the west side of the mountain, we haven't reconned that part yet. Maybe I'll get lucky and fall into a swimming pool."

"If you go, you'd better start early in the morning."

"Roger that," Price said.

"On the other hand, we can wait for rain."

Price looked at him blankly.

"I mean scrub the thing."

"No," Price said.

The sun failed behind the mountains and dusk came slowly, in pockets. Stringer opened a can of peaches and began to eat them, careful to catch the juice from the spoon. "The problem is that the harder you look for water, the sweatier and hotter and thirstier you'll get. And the more water you'll drink. You see the problem?"

"No choice," Price said. "And I'll take only a quarter of a canteen with me. How does your friend Steinberg manage it?"

"Beats me. Steinberg never said. He kept that information to himself, a state secret."

"Well, there's no choice."

"Not if we do what they want us to do."

"No choice there either."

"Well, yes and no. The rules are that on the ground, we're in charge. Those orders are technically suggestions. They're not do or die commands."

"To me they are," Price said evenly.

"I understand that. I was just telling you the terms of our employment. The job description. We live by them and so do they."

"Well, what the hell. These are *your* people."

"Right."

"It's fucked up, if you ask me." Price snapped his cigarette away and looked bleakly at Stringer. "What happens if you get a message. It'll be in code, you won't be able to read it."

"I can read it," Stringer said.

"They told me that you didn't have access to the codes."

"They told you wrong. How do you think I communicated the other times?"

Price shrugged and shook his head.

"Look. Don't think you're obliged to go. You're not. They've made a request, or a challenge if you like. You can take it either way. And we can accept it or not."

"I regard it as a command."

"*Bon voyage*," Stringer said.

"An order in the military is an order."

Stringer was about to reply, but did not. He sat silently and watched the valley darken, the shadows lengthen and become dark green. A light mist hung over the valley, shrouding it. The breeze, what there was of it, died. He lit a cigarette and raised the glasses to his eyes and watched the night come.

Price left the next morning with three empty canteens. Stringer could not convince him to leave the rifle and take his side arm. Price said he had no confidence in side arms. He promised to return by evening, and Stringer should on no account search for him if he did not return. Price emptied his pockets of everything except a package of cigarettes and matches, and was gone.

In the morning the road was deserted. At noon he watched a solitary figure walk quickly by. It could have been his imagination, or because he was waiting for it, but he thought the figure paused near the point where he'd disposed of the bodies of the two old men. In the heat of the day, they would begin to decompose. The scopes were not powerful enough to identify the figure beyond the fact that it was male and young, and walked in military cadence. No question: a scout. Stringer worried about the smell, it was possible that it could be mistaken for a dead animal. At first. Later, there would be no mistaking it for anything else.

At one in the afternoon he turned the radio on and sat with pad and pencil, waiting for a message. But there was nothing. For amusement, to break the boredom, he fiddled with the dial to see what he could get. Once, in similar circumstances, he'd managed to bring in WGN from Chicago, an atmospheric fluke. He'd caught the news and listened to disc-jockey talk before the sound faded. Usually he heard ships at sea or aircraft routinely broadcasting their positions or details of the weather. The radio crackled once, but yielded nothing. Then, clearly and urgently:

"Four this is Five. What is your location? Over."

"Five this is Four. Niner-two-niner-zero."

"I have that."

"We need two dust-off ASAP. Hot LZ."

"Roger that."

This would be a CO talking to a field unit. Stringer wondered where they were, whether south or east. The radio crackled again and fell silent. Then:

"Do you copy?"

"Fox Four this is Fox Five. Say again."

"I say, do you copy?" The voice was shaky and uncertain. Stringer could hear explosions in the background.

"Roger. Go ahead."

. . . .

"Fox Four I make your position niner-two-niner-zero. Will you confirm? Over."

. . . .

"Four this is Five. Confirm please."

. . . .

"This is Five calling Four. Over."

. . . .

"Five, Four come in. Over.

. . . .

"Come in at this time."

. . . .

"We are sending dust-off, Fox Four. Will you confirm ah your location."

. . . .

"Goddamn . . . this is Fox Five calling Fox Four. I make your location niner-two-niner-zero. Will you confirm at this time? This is Five. Come in, Four."

. . . .

"Fox Five calling Fox Three. Come in, Three."

"Five, this is Three."

"Have you been monitoring, Three?"

"That is correct."

"Well, check Four and get back to me. ASAP."

"Roger that, sir."

"I will loiter, Three."

"Back in five, Five. 'Bye."

There were more possibilities to that than Stringer liked to contemplate. One of the troubles was that all the messages were sent *en clair,* with no regard for the likelihood that the enemy had maps and monitors and language specialists. They liked to think of the enemy as ragtag groups of half-naked natives. In reality, this was a message sent to the enemy. A note lofted over the wall. Armies used machines stupidly and never took proper precautions. Too many radios, too many machines in general. As was well known, the machines took over from the men and operated on a logic of their own. Often they were more valuable than men, but sometimes they were not; they were more expensive and certainly more difficult to produce. There was a single computer expert who worked for Command, an expert who spent his days surrounded by metal and tape. This was Fitzhugh III, fiftyish, feisty, a nose like a headlight, no stranger to strong drink. He was a refugee from IBM and Burroughs, and controlled the machines by day and drank by night, gin over ice at the O Club. He was another of the men on contract, of indeterminate rank and authority; a technician. He'd been told that in the unlikely, indeed inconceivable, event of capture, he had the rank of colonel. A courtesy title, but respected by the Geneva convention. Fitzhugh III was not entirely satisfactory (his work habits were singular, as gaudy as Steinberg's were austere), and his efficiency reports were accordingly deplorable. He tried to explain the machines to Stringer, what they could do and what they could not do; he said they were very helpful in estimating difficulty and complexity. No good at all in solving simple problems — but, *mox nix*, there weren't any of those any more. A wizard, he was willing to work under adverse conditions. He was attracted to adverse conditions as a heliotrope to the sun. He drew strength from them; they confirmed his deepest prejudices. This was a positive — as Command once said — that tended to cancel out all the negatives. But Fitzhugh had respect for his metal and his tape.

Lost in thought, it was some seconds before Stringer realized that the sensor was buzzing.

He grabbed the glasses and looked into the valley, sweeping up the road from south to north. He did this with deliberation, very careful to note the smallest movement or irregularity. He looked into the hills beyond the road, looking for dust or smoke or signals of any kind. Then he put away the glasses and trained the telescope on the first sensor. He'd marked it precisely. Nothing unusual there. He moved the scope to the second sensor, along the road past the graves, then beyond. Nothing. He turned away and rubbed his eyes, listening to the buzzing, reminiscent of the irritating noise of an electric shaver. Christ, a click *that* strong; there would have to be something on the road, unless the machine was broken. And these machines did not break, Fitzhugh had assured him of that. And there was no evidence of malfunction. He went back again, first to the second

71

sensor, then to the first. There was no way of knowing which it was. No dust in the road or beyond, no evidence of convoy or of anything else. But it would pick up a moving vehicle a quarter of a mile away. Then the buzzing ceased.

". . . in trouble."

Stringer heard the radio, but did not listen to it.

". . . can't make out their position."

This was the field unit, Fox Three.

"This is Five. What do you propose?"

Stringer smiled, he was listening in spite of himself. Five was asking a subordinate to give the orders and plot the course of action. He was frightened to give the orders himself. Fox Five was afraid of error.

"Five, this is Fox Three. Send in a team."

"Roger."

Stringer switched off the radio and pulled the antennae down. A quarter of a mile beyond the second sensor the road curled away into the green hills and vanished. If there was to be a convoy, it would come from that direction. But there was no reason for a convoy to stop moving, let alone reverse course. It made no sense at all. But the sensor was silent. What it had heard was no longer moving, or had withdrawn.

Stringer remembered Fitzhugh's warning: "This dingus is sensitive, Stringer. It bruises easily. It's sensitive to dampness, you can't fuck around with it. Susceptible to malfunction, Stringer. It could trigger itself for no reason. That's something to remember, it's always a possibility. But it has very seldom happened, and that's a fact you should tuck away. Treat the machine with care, but demand that it perform; expect it. I have judged that the odds against screw-up are one in six hundred and twenty-two."

Crazy Fitz.

"How did you get that figure, Fitz?"

"The computer, asshole. It'll figure anything."

Stringer looked at the sensor's receiver, waiting. Then, faintly at first, the buzzing resumed. Stringer threw a switch on the radio and pulled the antennae high. He adjusted the dial and spoke quietly into the microphone.

"Dance Two this is Dance One. Stand by. Dance Two this is Dance One. I say again. Stand by."

"Dance One this is Dance Two. Eleven-fifty-five."

"Dance Two this is Dance One. Twelve-fifty-four. Stand by." Then Stringer paused the required fifteen seconds and spoke again, strongly and clearly. "Message commences:

11936   93843   22409   30468   11266   83297
69844   35942   46871   89203   33902   95326."

It was one message he knew by heart. Command would be ready to move now at a moment's notice.

Price had been gone six hours, a touching devotion to duty. He'd miss the dance. Something strange there, Stringer thought; something not quite right. Eager Price was taking heavy risk to find water in order to remain in hiding another week . . . at heavy risk. For a mistake, Command's, compounded. Someone else's error. But Price lived by the rules, as they all did. No other way to live, Price said. To Price, freedom was meaningless without rules. The rules determined the way they lived, the facts of their lives and nothing more. That was the mark of a pro, and one reason why young officers didn't do well in SAG. Too tight, they were obsessed with theory. They asked too many questions and were dissatisfied with the answers that they got. Paradoxically, they tended to optimism. Optimism, optimism.

Stringer, sweeping the road with his glasses, smiled.

For X, you were given Y.

Except of course for Steinberg.

Steinberg was a different case.

Another article altogether.

Steinberg made his own rules, and they were more severe than Command's. Steinberg believed in maximum attack, if Steinberg had been commanding they both would have gone in search of water. Or refused the assignment altogether. Steinberg's constitution was legendary, he had no need for food and little for water; he lived off the land. Steinberg demanded absolute silence on the march and required that any partner assigned to him be born under a harmonious sign. (Cancerous Steinberg favored Scorpios and Virgoans.) He carried a small chessboard, at night kneeling before it like a man at prayer. Hair in his eyes, scratching, smoking Camels, cracking wise.

I'm a hero of the Jewish people, Steinberg'd say.

The Malraux of Kew Gardens.

The wisest field-grade officer in the army.

The craftiest intelligence agent.

Checkmate, Steinberg!

Stringer laughed to himself, wishing that Steinberg

74

were there. They had fantastic luck, a string of successes. Steinberg and Stringer were the best in Special Action, Steinberg so deep inside the system he was almost invisible. Though technically a civilian, he'd acquired a provisional rank of lieutenant colonel; to tidy up the organization chart. Command had moved to replace him, a man too valuable to be risked in incautious assignments. But Steinberg'd hung on, knowing where the action was and insisting that he keep an eye on Stringer. There were rumors of powerful friends, he said he liked the work, and each time out devised new procedures. Drops, methods of search, concealment, codes, weapons. When they'd pull him back to base under protest, he took charge of the letter writing, explaining that he was a university man, literate, a product of the renaissance at the University of Chicago. He ordered up a desk sign:

> Steinberg, Lt. Col.
> Commanding Officer
> Literary Division

and wrote the KIA and MIA letters, fabricating dates, places, circumstances. Legal training helped, and sometimes he ghosted letters for Command on obscure but important war matters. The basic text for many of these was The Fowler Letter, a message written some years ago. Fowler was an officer said to be missing in action, though that was apparently far from the reality — to the extent that Command could understand the reality. They'd sent Fowler on a delicate and mysterious mis-

75

sion, and Fowler had not returned; all the circumstances were suspicious. An unmistakable figure of a man, Fowler was lean and thin-lipped and sarcastic in conversation. He tended to brood and was no man to cross. Command held the details very closely and distributed a misleading story; of course no one was fooled, and a kind of black humor surrounded Fowler's disappearance. More than once, Steinberg hinted to Stringer that there was more to the affair than met the eye, and thereafter insisted that judgment be suspended. At any event, Fowler's worried family was informed that he was missing and quite possibly dead, though some hope was not ruled out. The letter was a masterpiece of its kind, and Steinberg often cited its skillful use of the double negative; repeated attempts to assemble a straight story failed. The case and its implications still bedeviled Command.

Steinberg's rhythm: one month writing, one month in the field. The one justified the other. Of course he was missing now himself, despite the efforts to locate him. Poor Steinberg — no one knew, or was telling, where they'd lost him, a hint in itself of exotic missions. Steinberg's coordinates were not printed on any map, that much was for certain. Command would supply no information of any kind, a suspicious condition that gave rise to spirited speculation that Steinberg was detached and on his own. Not missing at all, but merely absent. It was possible, though not likely, that he was a captive. There had been no mention made of that by the enemy, but there seldom was; if true, Command would withhold the information. Steinberg would make a valuable prisoner, a repository of state secrets, and he had a healthy appreciation of life. He loved his own skin, it was impossible to imagine Steinberg without fingernails or genitals. Nothing capricious or romantic about Steinberg, although Command had mumbled drunkenly one night that he'd been touched by a bad hand. An involuntary volunteer. Command believed that Steinberg was less comprehensible than Stringer.

Stringer had been concentrating on the hum of the sensor for ten minutes, his eyes trained like guns on the road. He listened with mounting excitement and found himself grinning, his fingers beating an anxious tattoo on the ground. He smiled nervously: the footprints of the gigantic hound. Back in the mountains, where the road disappeared into the hills, he'd seen movement. It was so subtle, it might have been a breeze bending the trees. But it was not. It was a column of vehicles, he was certain of it. He took the microphone off the hook and laid it beside his hand. Just then he saw the first tank nose into view, so incongruous in the deep green thickness of the forest. This tank was a squat, light model, no more than ten tons; a single long gun swiveled left and right, like the antennae of an insect. Using the scope, Stringer could see the commander perched rigidly in the hatch, binoculars fastened to his eyes. The tank moved forward slowly and ponderously, creeping cautiously, an iron spider alone and vulnerable. Stringer drew himself up tight, holding his breath. Then he switched on the radio.

"Dance Two this is Dance One. Do you read?

"Dance Two reading."

Very prompt, Stringer thought. He waited for the code.

". . . eleven-fifty-three."

"Dance Two this is Dance One. Ten-fifty-two."

"We are reading."

"Dance One, *Tango*. I say again, *Tango*." He listened to the rustle of radio static, gripping the microphone hard in the palm of his hand. Then he heard the reply, a single silky word:

"Roger."

"I say again. Tango."

"Roger that, we are out."

"Tango" was code for commencing the attack. The strike would hit in thirty minutes, give or take a minute or two. The aircraft were guided by the sensors and by the coordinates Stringer had given them in the first message. Now he battened down the radio, tucked the antennae in the rear of the chassis, and covered it with a tarpaulin. He was taking no chances on a spotter in the convoy or, less likely, a wayward explosion.

Through the big scope he watched the commander in the lead tank, stiff in his weathered gray uniform. He wore no hat, and his hands were clasped behind his head like a prisoner. Stringer moved the scope back over the line of vehicles and men. They revealed themselves gradually from the forest, a reluctant chorus line moving stage center from the wings. The minutes ticked by. There were two trucks and another tank, a troop carrier, a third tank, three trucks, a mobile antiaircraft battery, two more trucks, a tank, another troop carrier, then a long line of men — foot soldiers — and two more trucks and a tank bringing up the rear. There were about three hundred soldiers by Stringer's estimate, a full battalion.

They were well-armed and appeared to march with good discipline, seasoned troops commanded by a veteran. The vehicles were old and painted dark green, and were moving very slowly over the narrow rutted road. The men walked with their rifles slung, tiny eddies of dust rising behind them.

Bucolic. The moment was drawn from a pastoral painting, provincial France in the nineteenth century, the green hills rising behind the sun, the clear blue sky, and the narrow road playing out before them. The road erupted as from a tunnel or hole in the earth, no beginning and no end; a mute lonely path suddenly in use, a traffic jam in the middle of the forest. The glasses brought the column up close and gave definition to the movement. The men swayed in their line of march. Without the glasses, the string of vehicles and men might have been anything, farmers on the way to market. Stringer lay on his back and turned his glasses to the pale sky, the northeast quadrant. If he was lucky, he'd spot the aircraft on the attack. But he would have to be very lucky.

He turned on his stomach and looked again at the convoy. This was his sixth — seventh? eighth? — mission. Waiting was a part of the drill, he'd been conditioned. It was routine now. The paraphernalia were familiar, the weapons, the radio, the scopes, the sensors of various kinds. And the concealment, there'd always been concealment. He hoped that Price was nowhere near the road; he hoped that Price had enough sense to move in the opposite direction, south, away from the road and the enemy convoy. But he could not be sure, because

Price was new at the game and didn't know all the customary precautions. He might have believed that a stream ran close to the road and was worth a chance . . . But that was Price's problem, it had nothing to do with anything else.

The convoy was now entirely exposed, strung out along the road like stones in a necklace. It looked as vulnerable and casual as the traffic on an American superhighway: soldiers sat on the tanks and troop carriers, their legs dangling loosely over the sides. Unaware, they had the illusion of complete security. Stringer thought it was odd that the offense was now so much more powerful than the defense: there were no moated castles any more. The design of tanks and trucks had not changed in fifty years, the armor plate was a bit thicker, the engines marginally more powerful, the gun calibers a bit wider. Nothing more. The tank was still an armored chariot; with all its ingenious improvements, it had the same goods and bads. The antiaircraft guns could reach higher, with greater force and somewhat greater accuracy. But the odds overall were with the offense, if the offense could achieve surprise; pilots in the high-flying aircraft were as safe as they would be approaching Des Moines. There was no equivalent danger, except of course to him, Stringer, who was acting as scout. He was hostage for the pilots and bombardiers and navigators of eight aircraft; he and Price. Stringer looked again at the long line of tiny machines and men, seventeen, eighteen vehicles, and a battalion of troops behind. The job would not be done today, they'd stay for a week all told; they'd fulfill the contract and destroy anything that could be seen or heard. There were enough supplies to last the battalion three months or more, food, ammunition, clothing, medical supplies, tents, maps, the lot. A valuable hit, worth the risk. Both sensors were buzzing, but Stringer did not notice them. The noise of the convoy did not carry to the top of the mountain, and he was straining to hear what sounds there were. The buzzing of the sensors was part of the mountain's noise, the wind and the rustle of the brush, and the creak of his clothing as he straightened his legs. The air hung, soft as fur, and Stringer began to squint, preparing himself. He buried his face in his hands when he saw the first explosion.

The lead tank simply disappeared, in a flash of fire and a puff of smoke. The bombs marched up the road like the drops of a thunderstorm pulled by wind. The bombs hit on the road and to both sides. In the first shower of bombs every third or fourth vehicle exploded. The column of men stood frozen for an instant, little lead soldiers held stationary in attitudes of movement. Then they broke to the left and right, diving for whatever cover there was. Soldiers fell over each other, tripped and dropped to the ground, and scrambled off the road. After the first wave of bombs there was a few seconds pause, and then a second wave, identical to the first. The trucks and tanks were pounded to rubble, and small fires started in the brush. The roar reached Stringer after the first tank exploded, a crescendo of sound that came at him in waves. But he did not look up.

The trucks were struck and flung off the road like toys, tossed crazily to each side of the road. The trucks were overturned and on their sides, on fire and charred. Ammunition began to explode, tracer bullets arching over the road in bright quick flashes; there was something comical and ineffectual about the tracers. No living thing was visible now, and after the second wave there was a third, then one fifty yards off target, the bombs falling harmlessly into the forest. A few men were back on the road now, sprinting back the way they had come. As they ran, bits of trees and earth were flung into the air, lifted high as if caught by slow-motion film. The men were knocked flat by the blast, thrown on their bellies like rag dolls. Then a fifth wave of bombs came fifty yards off to the other side, east; the bombardiers were bracketing the road. These were thousand- and two-thousand-pound bombs, the force of them enough to scramble anyone's brains; it was not necessary to be hit by the shrapnel. The shock of the blast smashed the blood vessels in the brain, causing hemorrhage and black-out. If the dead were found at all, they would be without clothing and probably without limbs. The force of the blast was enough to blow away fabric and tear skin.

The sixth and seventh waves were superfluous. There was no evidence any more of a convoy, only a mutilated road and a forest of craters. And dozens of fires, wisps of smoke and of course the smell. The bombs continued to fall although there was nothing left to kill. They fell as if by magic, because although the sky was clear there was no aircraft to be seen; no contrails nor telltale wings. There was an empty sky with bombs falling from it, the planes themselves long gone now.

Then there was silence, and Stringer raised his eyes.

He put his glasses to his eyes and surveyed the road, that part of it he could see. He had never witnessed or heard of a strike like that one. It was letter-perfect, exquisite in execution. Strategic bombing was usually not worth a damn, an error of a thousand meters could queer the entire mission. It was hellishly difficult to get the bombs on target from thirty seven thousand feet, and the target was usually moving. But this one was different, there was hardly a single wasted bomb.

He focused the glasses and saw two men staggering drunkenly on the road next to one of the smashed tanks. Poor bastards.

These were obviously sensors of a new kind, and now he understood the importance of the mission. The need to remain an extra week, and the order to get the sensors as close to the road as possible. And most important, Command had wanted an absolutely accurate bomb-damage assessment. They'd obviously keyed the sensors to the bombs in some way, the bombs guided not by the bombardier but by electrical impulses from the little black boxes. One flight of aircraft had done in five minutes what it would take a division of troops a month to do, *if they did it at all.* Foot soldiers could not destroy other foot soldiers. One unit could *damage* another, and often render it ineffective. But it could not annihilate. It did not have the power of annihilation.

There were two or three more, who'd emerged stumbling from the forest and now sat dumbly in the middle of the road, their heads in their hands. Some of them were naked, some half clothed; Stringer watched them through the glasses.

He felt remote. Perhaps that was the result of technology, the radios and the sensors. The thing existed for its own sake. He looked at his hands and saw they were shaking, but he was not afraid. Those who were on the road were two miles away, and it was unlikely they'd attempt to climb the mountain. They were in no shape to climb mountains or anything else. He was not afraid. He had his weapons, and his radio was still secure. He thought of the damage done by the planes, the complete success of the mission. It was as perfect as man could make it. But there would have to be a payment somewhere, there'd have to be some reaction. Some terrible swift sword. One never got something for nothing. Always you got something back, always. And there'd be one hell of a bill to pay now.

There were about a dozen of them in the road, some standing, most sitting or lying. Three or four still had their weapons. One of them was cradling it like an infant. They seemed unaware of where they were or what they intended to do. One of the men was administering first aid, probably morphine or some other pain-killer. The others were milling around like vagrants.

Stringer spoke into the microphone, wet with the sweat of his right hand.

"Dance Two this is Dance One."

"One this is Two." They were right there, not one wasted second. Models of military efficiency. Stringer could hear the excitement in Command's husky voice.

"Omega," Stringer said. "I say again. Omega."

"That's all there are?"

"Looks like it," Stringer said.

"How many were there?"

"Three hundred on foot. A battalion. Another hundred or so in the vehicles. You'll find it all written down, very detailed. There were seventeen vehicles. Probably more behind, although who knows. The others are probably waiting to make damn sure the planes are gone. That the coast is clear."

Price was silent for a moment. He was hunched down behind a rock, looking around it at the men on the road. He was shaking his head at the completeness of it.

"It was something to see all right, Price. Something to see. Those bastards there, I don't know how they survived. They've got to be scrambled as hell. If you'd seen it, you'd know what I mean."

"I felt it, Stringer."

"You had to see it."

The dozen men on the road were all seated in a circle. They were trying to figure out what to do now, trying to plot the future. Where to go, what precautions to take. They were armed, all of them, though some were without clothing. But they were not entirely sane, Stringer could judge that by their jerky movements.

"I suppose we ought to think about the possibility that they'll wander up here."

"Not a chance," Stringer said. "They couldn't walk ten feet in a straight line."

"But there will be others."

"I expect there will be. And I suspect they'll have suspicions of one kind or another."

"We'll wait and see."

"We've got the water to stick it out. Five full canteens now. Thanks to you, we've got enough water for another week of this."

"Sorry about that, Stringer."

Price was grim, he was sorry he'd missed the strike. From two miles away he'd heard it and felt it, but he hadn't seen it. He wanted to. He'd never seen one, although he'd read hundreds of eyewitness reports. But he wanted to witness it himself, his own retina registering the damage. No matter how clear the reports were, they missed certain details. Military reports were not graphic, they were analytical. Where he'd been, he was very close. For a few moments he thought he was much too close, but then the explosions stopped. Rolling thunder, suddenly ended; the forest quiet again. All of it happened in half a minute or less, one continual roar and heave. One had to see it to understand the energy, the palpable random craziness of it. Suddenly Price smiled, focusing his glasses on the road below.

"Well well well."

"I see them," Stringer murmured.

"How many do you make?"

"Thirty, thirty-five men. One truck. No, two."

"You're right about the others, Stringer. They aren't moving worth a damn, look at them. They're just sitting in a circle. Christ, *look at that*. You can feel it, even up here. Scrambled eggs."

Stringer looked at the men in the road and suddenly he was very tired. He slumped against the rock, rubbing his eyes. He took a long drink of water, the taste of it rancid in his mouth. He thought he would go to sleep, let Price handle it for the moment. Price was alert and eager. He fished around in his knapsack and brought out the paperback. "I'm bushed. I'm taking a nap, Price."

The other looked at him with a small, quizzical smile.

"It's all right, Price. It won't be for long. I'm not going anywhere. Just over there. Just to the other side, away from that. You let me know if anything happens."

"I'll wake you when they move."

"They're not moving anywhere."

Stringer took his book and walked away fifty yards, along the summit ridge. He propped himself against a rock and opened the book, the pages cool to his touch. From where he was seated he could see the road and the men on it, milling about in unmilitary formations. The road was littered with smoking vehicles and the dead, the trash of war. The forest on both sides was smoldering, smoke without fire. The day was failing, the shadows lengthened, long arms reaching across the valley. Looking up suddenly, he saw the daytime moon, very pale, almost invisible against the light blue sky. The moon's presence was vaguely comforting to him, a link to the past and the future, a familiar witness to things that had gone before. For the moon, there were no surprises. But this was as bad as anything he had ever seen. Stringer could not imagine worse. Perhaps worse in degree, if that had meaning: but tempest was measured in essence.

"Good evening, sir," he muttered. If he'd had a hat, he would have tipped it; but he had no hat. The moon lay low against the sky, small and flat as a dime. "General Moon."

Stringer thought that the moon assumed various personalities, depending on the circumstances of observation. Moon was a skillful character actor. Tireless lover, wise philosopher, dreamy poet, creative general. In the role of general, Moon would've won medals for valor and endurance. The Croix de Guerre, the Iron Cross, the Medal of Honor, the Order of Lenin, the Victoria Cross, the maiden's hand in wedlock. Whatever honors were available. Witness to Thermopylae, Jena, Gettysburg, Gallipoli, Smyrna, Iwo, and now this. In the annals of war, this particular engagement would be known as the Airstrike at Coordinates 8346–1343, numbers on military maps. General Moon would be ordered to supply his appraisal, the after-action report, in concise and objective summary — although it was a single battle in a very long war. A war that some thought would persevere forever, the fighting now heavy, now light, but always there — always to turn up again, dapper in a new suit of clothes, eager to please, an agreeable guest at any occasion. A war with us wherever we are, whenever we open our eyes and look upward. For the rest of time. Stringer smiled, and saluted his companion.

The moon became stronger as it rose. Presently the sun's rays were lost to view altogether, and the road and its wreckage faded. The moon was alone, solitary in the sky. But by then Stringer was asleep, his head on his chest, the paperback book neatly folded in his lap. And Price watching him from a distance, still smiling.

Before he was fully awake he heard Price talking into the microphone. The radio's electrical hum filled the air, charged it. He replaced the book in his knapsack, pushing

88

it down out of sight. It was dark now, and he noted glumly that the moon was high and full. He took the pack and his weapon and walked over to Price.

"Command wants one more run, and then we can get out of here. We can go home, Stringer."

"Bully for us." Stringer was still half asleep, he was not fully registering.

"Their intel says that another convoy is due tomorrow or the next day. A bigger convoy than this one. So that means getting two more black boxes down there. And doing it now. At night. Command says he appreciates our efforts."

Stringer took the night glasses and looked at the road. He could make out the men, scattered along its edge, asleep. They were not well camouflaged, but there were no lights of any kind.

"How well do you remember the road?"

Stringer nodded. "Well enough."

"And the route down?"

"I can get down," Stringer said.

"It's 2300 hours right now. I think the time to move is about midnight. That moon will be helpful, for part of the trip it'll be bright as day. Of course that cuts both ways, doesn't it? But on the whole a net plus."

"Sure."

"You've got to get within a hundred meters of the road, then move up about a mile and plant the second box. It doesn't have to be quite as precise as the first two. It shouldn't be too difficult. There's no reason for them to have scouts out."

"Oh shit no. No reason at all. Why would they want

scouts out? They've just been knocked to hell by half the air force, by planes that came from nowhere. They've got to figure that's coincidence, right Price? Just a little coincidence of war, a matter of guessing the right coordinates on a war map and sending half the air force to bomb it . . ."

"Stringer?"

"Get it through your professional army head that there is no such thing as coincidence! Coincidence does not exist! Good luck and bad luck exist. Smarts and dumbs exist. Coincidence does not exist, no." Stringer thought that they would have scouts and everything else out and awake. Goddamned awake. At least that is what he would have if he were commanding. If he were the lieutenant colonel in charge he'd reckon that there were some unfriendlies in the area. Where? Two places, one of two. On the mountain ridge to the east or the ridge to the west. Those were natural lookouts. Now, if he were the lieutenant colonel commanding he would not send a patrol. No. Because the patrol could be spotted easily enough and avoided. Patrols made noise. So that was pointless, unnecessary. And those people never did an unnecessary thing. The idea would be to throw out listening posts to encircle their bivouac, stakeouts of three men each; well-trained men who knew how to listen and keep quiet. Who would not smoke or talk or do anything to disclose the position. They would sit and wait for intruders. If the lieutenant colonel commanding were lucky, he would find the trail to the east ridge. He would see that feet had beaten it down here and there, that it had been used. But he would not be absolutely certain of that, because Stringer had been careful; he would have suspicions, though, and those would sustain him. "How exactly did they appreciate our efforts."

"Just that."

. . . .

"That we'd shortened the war." Price smiled.

. . . .

"Our mission accomplished."

"Yes." Stringer lit a cigarette.

". . . and the war shortened."

"Oh really? By how much? Two and a half minutes? Perhaps two and a half hours. What is two and a half hours subtracted from infinity? You've forgotten, Price. This is the war that goes on forever and ever. This is the endless war."

"Well, that's lucky for you, Stringer." Price laughed. "You've got time. Time to move. Time to get off your ass. To stop talking and start moving. Time to show your stuff."

four

THE PATH was lit by moonlight, but Stringer knew the way. He intended to move as deftly and economically as the scout Daniel Boone, all he lacked was the legend, the coonskin, the muzzle-loader, and the Indian enemies. And Lord Byron to write the verses. Scouting was an ancient military tradition, though not particularly honorable. Well yes, it was honorable in its way.

Stringer felt for the black boxes in his shirt and the pistol on his shoulder and skipped cautiously forward. This strange country, no one knew its history; it existed in a historical vacuum, its kings and princes as stiff and lifeless as alabaster statues. The river beyond the mountain had a name that translated river-beyond-the-mountain. This was once a fertile region, though there were now no signs of cultivation. Stringer supposed that the river was similar to the Rappahannock in Virginia, its banks yielding up old bones and weapons. Evidence of conflict, and therefore of history. Evidence of passion: the land was worth fighting for. This river-beyond-the-mountain looked counterfeit, the Rappahannock was a real river, lazy and placid and murderous; it was the bloody spine of the American Civil War. A man could write a history of the Civil War from its banks: the second battle of Bull Run, Chancellorsville, Fredericksburg, Brandy Station, Kelly's Ford, the Wilderness Campaign. They had all been fought within sight of the gentle Rappahannock, the river defining the boundaries of the battlefields. In 1863 the whipped northern army struggled across it after losing seventeen thousand men at Chancellorsville. From a distance, with the green hills rising around it, the river-beyond-the-mountain looked like the Rappahannock near Front Royal. Probably a hundred years ago there were inhabitants enough to make a war and keep it going. Some comfort, Stringer thought; he could look on his own war as a second Wilderness Campaign, except that in this country it was one on one. Grant could've used Boone in that singular offensive: he lost sixty thousand men before it was over.

In a difficult place, Stringer liked to set his mind free. To let it poke among the debris of his memory. Where had he first heard of the Rappahannock and its mysteries, he was no student of the Civil War? From Boone, of course. Boone the statistician and historian, poor Boone. He'd made a study of conflict and weapons, from hop-

94

lites to commandos. Among his other researches, many of them civil and quite pacific in nature.

Daniel Boone, Douglas Boone. Now that was a story, compelling enough to distract the subconscious and keep it occupied. Boone, brilliant student at the University of Chicago during Stringer's year in residence. Was onto Riesman and the others before the crowd. Boone had a center of gravity, he was a very lonely but brilliant student. He lived alone in a dormitory on the Midway, down the hall from Steinberg, earning part of his tuition as a research assistant. Boone researched statistics, hence his intimate knowledge of the Rappahannock River, its tributaries, and the deaths in that vicinity. And one day he slid into a depression from which he never recovered, and for all Stringer knew he was still in the state hospital south of Springfield. The family never mentioned Boone's fate, he was a student who'd disappeared. A *brilliant* student, psychiatric counseling was of no benefit. Boone could not cease weeping, and of course he could supply no answers. He told someone that each tear was a fact — an uncharacteristically romantic remark from Boone, who was thought to be coldly analytical and emotionally dry. That was how his reputation flourished at the University of Chicago, though his critics claimed he was never as brilliant as his reputation. A seminal student, monastic in outlook, Boone arrived on the Midway from an army separation depot in the state of Washington. He'd spent his obligatory two years in the army, doing duty in Korea during the war there. Lucky Boone, he never heard a shot fired in anger; he was a staff man, an

95

analyst in the G-2 shop (intelligence). He did not find the army to his taste. *Mindless*, he called it, an artless clanking ancient machine gone out of control. Gentle Boone wrote a monograph of his experience with intelligence in the army, who collected it and how, and what happened to the information. The document made melancholy reading.

At the University of Chicago, he'd put that behind him, and all was well for a number of years. Then, like a child tumbling down a sand dune, Boone slipped into a depression from which he could not rise. The doctors at the hospital downstate said that no recovery was possible. To spare the family, they told them that Boone was a victim of his own brilliance. He saw too deeply, in too many different directions; he'd leaned over the precipice. That gave the family something to hang on to, and they lived on in the apartment building in Homewood, Illinois, happily unaware of the terms of their boy's existence. He was the first crazy that Stringer knew, a tangible visible victim of the intellectual renaissance at the University of Chicago.

He told his wife about Boone and Steinberg, and the good times they'd had; Stringer was eighteen and Steinberg was twenty-one. Boone was twenty-three. It never occurred to either of them to ask the ex-soldier about his army career and the war in Korea; the war in Korea was scrupulously remote. Stringer took his wife to see Boone, the last month they were together in Chicago. They drove for four hours to the hospital downstate, after arranging a visit by letter to the authorities. Boone met them in the visitors' room, a gaunt gray man with a

96

sweet smile and a high-pitched laugh. Stringer's wife had brought him a box of candy, which he handed to the guard. Then they went for a walk on the lawn.

Stringer's lithe blond wife talked quietly to Boone. Did he have enough books? Were there movies in the hospital? What movies did he like best? When did he first come to know Stringer? Lightly: did he think at all about the university?

Boone was slow to reply.

"Do they let you listen to music?"

"No."

"That's outrageous," Stringer's wife cried, shocked.

"Yes, isn't it?"

"What can we do to help?" Stringer's wife asked, after a half hour's walk on the lawn. Stringer was silent, trailing along behind, like minor nobility following the royal suite. "You tell us, and we'll do it." She put her arm on his, but he jerked it away. She was near tears. "Perhaps a box of food from time to time."

"You shouldn't have come," he said finally.

Stringer, shattered by the surroundings, didn't answer.

"Mistake," Boone said.

"We wanted to come," Stringer's wife said gently.

Boone drifted away from them a little and came up against a tree. There were others on the lawn, sitting on benches and on the grass. Someone was playing a transistor radio, bouncy popular music floated across the lawn. Boone awkwardly leaned his head against the bark of the tree, rubbing it.

"Boone, you're molting," Stringer said, desperate for a laugh. He said it with college inflections. But this Boone bore only slight resemblance to the one he'd known. This Boone was a darker man. It was as if he were talking to an older brother or a distant cousin. Boone continued to scrape his head on the bark of the tree.

An orderly drifted within range.

"Come with us now," Stringer said quietly. His friend was beginning to bleed at the temples. He took Boone's arm and tried to lead him away from the tree. For a frail man, Boone was surprisingly strong. "You'll hurt yourself, Boone."

"Douglas?" It was Stringer's wife.

"I've tried everything," Boone said. He ducked his head as she came closer and put her arm around his shoulders. They stood there for a moment, three of them in an embrace. There was a faint smear of blood on her white sleeve. Stringer was the first to disengage, his wife's gentleness moved him; he put his arm around her waist and could feel her trembling.

"You come with us," she said.

No, Stringer thought. No, no.

"The works," Boone said, looking at her. His body had gone slack.

The orderly moved away and was hovering now around a group of five women. He was a husky orderly with a benign expression on his institutional face. White coat, black shoes, heavy eyeglasses, close-cropped hair, powerful arms.

"Knives razors sticks stones broken bottles a length of rope shoelaces my own hands a pillow a dictionary . . ." Boone stopped and shook his head, and then his body began to shake. Stringer could not tell if he was laughing or crying. There were no tears.

"Douglas?" Stringer's wife still had her arms around his shoulders. She pressed up close against him, looking into his eyes.

"Now tree bark!" he said loudly. "Fucking tree bark!"

"Boone . . ."

"I can't fucking kill myself no matter what I fucking do!" Boone was shouting, and the orderly looked over in their direction. There was a problem with the five women, an argument of some kind, and he was undecided what to do. Stringer heard raised voices and waved the orderly away.

"Boone, let's get something to eat."

"Eat! I tried to fucking eat myself to death a year ago. Hah! Hash! Stuffed fucking hash down my throat. To fucking plug the hole. No air in or out. A vacuum. Christ, I couldn't do it! Stringer, doesn't a soul have the fucking right —"

"Douglas, Douglas . . ." Stringer's wife had her face buried in his chest. She was crying and Boone had his arm around her. He was looking at Stringer and shaking his head, subdued now, muttering unintelligibly. Then Stringer saw Boone as he had been. Boone standing before a fireplace, confidently jiggling coins in his pocket; Boone striding down a university sidewalk, swinging a book bag. Surrounded by a university, drowned in it; suffocating in it; living it, loving it. The books, the lectures, the look of the quadrangle. The past casting light on the future, all of it knowable. But the winners wrote the histories, Boone. The losers had no access to pen and ink. Wouldn't you say that colors the view? One fog substituted for another, fair enough. Let us not enter into a discussion of virtue as it is seen from occupied thrones. But Boone didn't understand, and began his long slide into the depression. A depression in the earth, and the deeper he probed the colder it got; the center of the earth, he professed to believe, was cold and dark as a stone sunk in Iceland.

Boone was silent now, he had nothing more to say. Stringer's wife relaxed her clumsy grip, and the three of them walked back to the main building, strolling very slowly at dusk. Stringer remembered the moment exactly: at the twin doors his wife kissed Boone on the cheek and took his hand. She told him they would return, sometime. He had to remember that he had friends and was not forgotten. He was to write or call them if there was anything they could do. Meanwhile, she would think about him; he would be in her thoughts. Sweet Boone, she said, stay well. Blankly, without comprehension, he looked at her beautiful wet face. Then he turned away and walked off. They shook hands at the door, and Boone went on inside without another word. He left Stringer's wife standing alone, without a sign or word of any kind. There were two orderlies with him now, and as he moved up the long flight of stairs he looked like a condemned man being led to the gallows. Except that there were no gallows in the state hospital. There was only his room, with the door and the two windows; and the glass in the windows out of reach.

Stringer took care now and snapped his mind back

to the present. He picked his way down the hill, moving five steps and pausing one. Moving five, and pausing again. He watched for movement in the shadows. The pistol was heavy on his shoulder, the black boxes slick with sweat. His head began to ache, a low dull throb. He wondered where they were and when they would come. How many listening posts they had and how many men in each listening post. They were very good at that, very cunning. Excellent discipline. He was glad he'd eaten and slept well, but he wished his headache would go away. The moon was high and full, there was too much light. He thought then that it was certain that they would come tonight, singly or in pairs. They had all the evidence they needed and would be compelled to investigate. Stringer drew back, watching himself, careful to keep a low silhouette.

Douglas Boone. Their lives intersected at odd points. From time to time, after the one visit to the hospital, he'd had word of Boone. The news would come from a friend, announcing receipt of a series of letters, written by hand, prolix, confusing. Boone, stashed away in the hospital, wondered where his friends were, why it was that in his institution he was surrounded by strangers. At the university, they'd had a community — classes to attend, places to meet. They'd had a circle. The university administration was not neutral: his enemies were pulling the strings that kept him caged, and therefore alive. That in itself, he wrote in one letter, was cruel and unusual punishment; a court, any court, would strike it down. But the letters, fervent and disjointed, indicated no desire to escape. He was what he was, a small neat man seated in a wooden chair at a desk in the corner of a cell. Locked up, locked in. Knowledge was no help, brilliance held him back. They supplied him with a flimsy pencil, one inch in length, and long sheets of ice-white paper. Dear Boone, Dear Stringer. They began a correspondence, Boone's hand a childish scrawl, sometimes he'd draw a picture at the end. A scowling face, an object of some kind. The first sentence signalled atmospheric conditions. *My room is sunny today. Outside it is raining. There's snow on the windowsill, and a bird is frozen in flight.* The letters' last sentences were general statements. *I write a letter a day. I have a book. No facts today.* Stringer's first letter, which went unanswered for a year, dealt with their lives together at the University of Chicago. The Rockefeller Chapel, the Midway, the Compass Bar, long evenings licking envelopes for Adlai Stevenson's presidential campaign. The university went squarely for Adlai — its New Testament prophet, its man of goodwill, patriarch of the human family, its living library of great thoughts. Stevenson lost, thank God. No one at the university wanted anything to do with power or its effects (as Stringer reminded Boone). No moral there, only another demonstrable fact. Boone was an enthusiastic worker, sincere in his admiration for the governor. Stringer and Steinberg were bone-idle, sunshine soldiers. But Boone's letters explained nothing, they sought to conceal the causes of his illness. Stringer made no sense of them. A funny place to live, the 1950s: it was a number on a house on a tree-shaded street in a small town, driven like a stake into the heart of the country.

Halfway down the path, Stringer paused for five minutes. He concentrated on his hearing, his head bent. The moon kept watch, no friend to him now; the moon was aiding the enemy. Stringer's instinct told him to advance cautiously, his enemies were near him. He was not alone. Stringer bent his head to the ground, listening. His senses were alive and trembling, something was wrong. He moved off the path into the underbrush. Something touched his head and was gone. A night animal of some sort, disturbed by his movement. The full moon threw queer shadows, the milky light infiltrating the forest. He knew he had another mile to travel before he reached the road. He was forced to hustle and decided to give it another thirty seconds on his watch; thirty seconds and then scoot. Stringer was lying flat, faced downtrail, the heavy pistol cradled in his palm. Something fluttered ahead of him, then he saw one of them, moving up toward him. There was just the one, small and brittle in the moonlight; a figure hardly bigger than a boy's. Dressed entirely in black, advancing in a good loose-limbed crawl; Stringer heard the creak of muscles and the soft sounds of breathing. He'd been well taught. Stringer's hands went cold, the other was now no more than twenty yards away. He stopped then and lay absolutely still, his face pressed against the earth. It was the motion of a suspicious and careful man. Stringer thought: no noise, no shooting, no killing unless absolutely necessary. He'd follow the enemy's cardinal rule, never do an unnecessary thing. Never gesture, *act*. But the other one was crawling again, closer, and Stringer's hand tightened on the trigger of his pistol. Christ, his instincts were good. He had the best instincts of anyone. He had to remember that, to trust what he felt; to take all the normal precautions, but in the last analysis to trust what he felt. What he knew.

Stringer braced himself, his man was now five yards away and moving up the path. They were parallel, to hit him Stringer would have to dart quick as a cat. He had no purchase on the ground, his feet were splayed out behind him. His man would have warning, the odds would not be equal; Stringer was bigger, but this other one was younger and quicker. Stringer could smell him now, a thick sweet scent; the intruder stank. He saw rope-soled sandals, a bracelet of elephant hide, and a knife in one hand. Slow, inexorable movement. The enemy's eyes did not shift. Mind numb, Stringer concentrated on the man's motion, the rhythm of his crawl. He thought then that he would let him go. Let him go on up the path, Price could deal with him at the summit: a nocturnal meeting at the summit. Price was awake, he prided himself on acute hearing. Total control, nimbleness. Stay alert to stay alive, Price said. Now he would have the opportunity to put that into effect, he'd be able to test the validity of it under combat conditions. Stringer watched his man move away, then lay very still. They both waited. There was just the one, and Stringer doubted there would be another. In the trade this was known as a suicide run, and they would send their very best man. It was important to them to know where the enemy was. This was a one-man operation, and if it could not be completed alone, there would be no chance in pairs. So Price could deal with that. It was Price's problem now. Stringer watched his man glide away, he saw the soles of the sandals retreat. Presently the other was out of sight. Stringer waited five minutes, then scuttled down the slope very quickly. He reckoned that the enemy would have a listening post ten minutes away.

Price spun forward, clutching his stomach. Pains, fever. He coughed twice, then held his breath. His lungs and stomach burned, and tears sprang to his eyes. It was the foul water, the halizone hadn't been potent enough. Now something rotten was in his stomach, and it would take a day or two to expel it. Bad luck, Price thought; bad, stupid, rotten luck. The waves of nausea hit him like fists, he gagged and retched. Nothing to do but wait it out, for however long it took. But God he was sick. Sicker than he'd ever been, he thought. He longed to sleep, but he knew that was wrong. That violated every rule he'd been taught. He could not sleep even if he should, and he certainly should not.

They'd done the first part of the job damn well. Command would be pleased, there'd be a long leave in prospect for them both. A leave for him, and money for Stringer. A medal for Stringer, and a quick promotion to major for him, when this tour ended. He thought in the beginning that it was a mistake, working for the civilians. But there were no distinctions, really, except in the procedures. Some of the civilians were soldiers on leave, and some of the soldiers were civilians on TDY. Only the procedures differed, civilians were looser and less disciplined. Loose liberals, their politics indicated their behavior. No *there* there. They did not understand hard, straight lines of command and control, with responsibility evenly proportioned.

Another wave of nausea hit him then, and he bent forward, moaning, his hand over his mouth. He'd been ahead of them always, beginning at Culver and continuing through the Academy and through Benning and the first and second tours. Always at the head of the class, the club, the team, the squad, the platoon, the company. Now he was head of this, too, except that Stringer did not take orders. Stringer did what was necessary, and nine times out of ten — or more, give him that, he was still alive, after all — these agreed with the formal orders from the chain of command. Stringer was capable, but Price wished he had some young stud out of the airborne or ranger school. One simple tough PFC would be preferable to Stringer. The sullen bastard. But competent. No denying that. He had an instinct for anything out of the way, private, stealthy. He was a natural for it, a damned natural. Strange then that he had no use for leadership. Leadership: that was what it was about.

Price moaned, the pain was worse. A bad one, the worst one yet. The pain was like a knife in the belly, cutting deep, hurting so. He dozed, after swallowing a dose of paregoric. He dozed with his eyes open, one hand on his burning stomach, the other on the trigger of his rifle. He watched the trail, its darkness looming up at him; it was dark as a tunnel in hell. He thought about the army, his life as an army man, son of an army officer. It was to live differently than other men, other Americans; it was a different atmosphere. The pledge of allegiance. Grace at meals. Obedience. To retire at colonel was the worst thing; he'd watched his father collect a pension. His honorarium, like the gold watch given to a railroad brakeman. So now he and the old lady lived in Florida, the old man drank and sold real estate, and the old lady attended garden clubs. Price knew that his father had been scared for twenty years and wondered about causes. The war had scared him, that much was certain; it was simple fright, nothing complicated about it at all. So now he was able to keep track of his boy, following in the military tradition. It was living within a form, inside an equation. The family was always up at five-thirty, rising to the sound of reveille. Bugles, for Christ's sake, pulling them from their beds like magnets. He remembered what Stringer said, that an army officer was like a stage performer, an entertainer; a musician drawing support and nourishment from the audience. Except that for an army officer the support and nourishment were of a different kind, and the audience was involuntary and unpaid. It had not paid its own admission.

Damn Stringer. Negative. Unpatriotic. Selfish. Cynical.

Price wanted his own company, maneuvering out in the open.

Someone had to do it, he thought. That was what the colonel said, around the breakfast table in the mornings. Someone had to do it and no one gave a damn until the time when it had to be done. Then the support was everywhere, and the civilians and their goddamned newspapers blew smoke at you until you couldn't see clearly. General officers, walking with arched spines caused by the embrace of politicians. Civilization's first line of defense, the politicians having failed; first and last for the matter of that, there being no other. Brave men. Everything depended on brave men and the army system itself, the book by which soldiers lived. Now he was sitting on top of a fucking mountain because of all that, although he'd done it on his own hook. No. It was the way he'd lived, the things he'd heard. He'd never seen another way. Unlike Stringer, who'd had a dozen ways to move; Stringer still had all his moves. Stringer'd aged without complications and without direction. No one preaching at him, no one reminding him of tradition and responsibility. T and R, the colonel said late at night, after drinks. His red face and white hair, crow's feet at the corners of his moist eyes. The colonel: that's what it's all about, and it's a thing you can take pride in. A ruined life, a ruined liver, and unexpressed anger. Anger coiled in the gut, that's what the colonel had. But he also had a good deal of pride in the army, which had been good to him. Very.

The thing went in, the knife's blade reaching to his throat, inside his stomach, burning, thrusting up. Hot, he was sick as hell. His own hands were poised in a vise, and his mind went black then. He squeezed, his hands hard and rough as iron. As he died he squeezed harder, relying then not on instinct but on discipline. At the end there was no escape for either of them.

The moon was now his friend. Stringer moved off the trail to his right. He knew where they were now, and the knowledge made him bold. It was going to work out all right after all. The underbrush was not thick, and he was able to slip around and under the larger bushes and trees. He was moving very easily now, he decided to save his concentration. The way Stringer dealt with fear was to think of something else, to put his mind into another place and time and try to remember the details. Or misremember the details, he was never sure which. He continued to think of Boone, as if a reconstruction of those events was a thing of value, a key to the mint.

He was appalled and horrified when Steinberg informed him.

"Down the pipe," Steinberg'd said.

"Why? How?"

"Nobody knows the answer to that, except Boone and he's not talking," Steinberg said.

"Where is he?"

"In a hospital. Not here."

"Could you see it coming?"

"I think I could. There were signals. Now, with the benefit of hindsight. Hindsight's a valuable thing."

"He was working hard."

"Very, very hard. But I don't think he knew what he wanted to do. I think that bothered him. He felt an obligation. I think that was one of his troubles."

Stringer remembered that Steinberg was arch, almost amused at the terrible turn of events. Steinberg seemed to think it confirmed a private vision, and not at all the worst of those. Boone as proof. Boone as symptom of the future. Boone who never did a mean thing to a living soul, crazy as a loon. "Well, can we visit?"

"Boone has no visiting hours, or so the family says. He's in isolation, the doctors think that's best. For him to grapple with his difficulties."

He and Steinberg were sitting at the bar in the Compass, drinking Meister Brau and watching the clock.

Midafternoon in mid-September, cool and damp inside the bar; the scent of beer and cigarette smoke, sunlight spilling through the front windows, the bartender crisp and white behind the bar. The academic year had just begun.

"He'll be the first of a long line," Steinberg said.

"Bullshit, Steinberg."

"No. You wait. You'll see."

"Bullshit."

"It's a virus, like the plague."

"An epidemic, I suppose," Stringer said.

"They've already cleared the things from his room. The books, the records, the prints. Boone's Van Gogh prints are now in the possession of the parents, ditto the Stravinsky and the Brahms. It's a vacant room now, except for the bed and the dresser and the view of the Midway. Boone's view, Stringer. It's still there."

At the rear of the Compass there was a snooker pool table. He heard the tiny balls roll and click and bounce off felt. *Thuckthuck.* It was very cool inside the bar. The barman was bored, inspecting his fingernails in the dark light; he was a graduate student in the history of art.

"Shall we write him a letter?"

"Well, now. Just what would we say?" Steinberg warmed to the subject. "Hope you're released from the loony bin? Hope you get your head straight? Hope you chase away the demons? No, Stringer. Bad idea. Nothing to say that would do good, much that might do harm. Never do an unnecessary thing, Stringer. That's the key to it in this business. Boone needs to be left alone."

"I'll write anyway."

"You do that."

Stringer signaled the barman, who drew two fresh draughts of beer. They arrived, the foam slipping over the edge of the glass. They looked better than they tasted.

"It might be time to quit this place, you know."

"Finish the beer first."

"I mean the *university*, Stringer. The university. It might be time to say the hell with books and enter ourselves elsewhere. A new sweepstakes. Perhaps that is what it was with Boone, a question of action."

"To find the action."

"Yes. Like that."

"And where do you suppose we might do that? A roustabout in Texas, perhaps. The money's good, the weather's terrible. Is that action enough for you?"

"One possibility."

"The others?" Stringer was talking without listening. The atmosphere of the bar had taken him in. He felt languid, warm and serene inside the darkness. He was still thinking about Boone.

"Would it be a gas to join the army?"

"*Christ!*"

"Or the intelligence services."

"Steinberg, that's insane. The army? And what the Christ are the 'intelligence services'?"

"You're other-directed, Stringer. You cannot see inner possibilities in things. You cannot see how disaster can be turned to advantage. Let's do something unique. Something . . . that no one's done before."

"Tell it to Boone."

"I did, once."

Steinberg was making wet circles with his glass bottom. One ring overlapped another, until he had a dozen of them on the surface of the bar; now, years later, Stringer remembered the look of the place, the smell and feel of it. A place as familiar as home. Same records on the Wurlitzer, same jokes pinned to the bulletin board back of the bar. WYBMADIITY. He wondered if the Compass was still alive and thriving. Somewhere in the rear of the room a telephone rang.

"It's an idea," Steinberg said.

"A bad one."

"I don't think there's anything more to be gained here. I think the Midway is out of gas. I think we're in a bus that's broken down. We simply haven't recognized it yet, our eyes aren't accustomed to the scene. The leading edge of a singular cultural event. Perhaps we'll be the first on our block to see it clearly and in focus, past and future as one. A leading edge of our very own, Stringer."

"You're full of shit."

"Well, I've got the answers anyway."

Steinberg was like that, he answered one statement with another. He thought he was onto something, and would not now let go.

"Drinking gives me great pleasure, Stringer."

"I can see that."

"Boone did not drink, that may've been one of his troubles. One of his many difficulties. How does the army, or something like it, strike you?"

"Badly," Stringer said.

"Well, of course you're not involved."

"No."

"I may do it. We'll have to see. We'll have to see how bad things really are. What do you want for yourself, Stringer? An insurance agency? You've been conditioned, you're another one of Pavlov's spaniels." Steinberg was speaking softly. "Let's pay up and see if we can escape this place without settling our debts. I mean the *university*, Stringer."

"Why do that?"

"It'll get us off on the right foot. As outlaws."

Steinberg was watching a girl sitting alone at the end of the bar. She was dressed in the fashion of the day, a sweater and gray Bermuda shorts, a gold bracelet on her wrist and a red tam perched on her head. She was talking to the bartender and sipping from a rum and Coke, her feet crossed on the bottom rung of the barstool. Her hair was short and brushed back, she had the look of a mischievous tomboy. Steinberg stared at her.

"That girl is in my sociology class."

"Is she good at it?" Stringer was dreaming again.

"How does one know? There are a hundred and fifty students in this class, which is conducted, mind you, in an auditorium. No questions, no answers. She seems attentive. Is awake. Takes notes."

"Nice ass," Stringer muttered.

"I would say that. She's a notetaker, though."

The girl's hand reached out and touched the bartender's wrist. They were laughing together, the bartender leaning over the polished surface. Stringer remembered the way she cocked her head when she laughed, and the lightness and the softness of her arms.

Steinberg was frankly staring, and this embarrassed Stringer; everyone had a right to privacy. But the girl and the bartender never noticed: their eyes touched, held, and strayed away. The bartender was holding the girl's middle finger as if it were a precious gem. She lightly brushed the bones of his hand. They smiled at each other, silent; Steinberg rapped on the bar for service. Stringer remembered that they left shortly thereafter, and in a week had quit the university, heading south in Steinberg's car.

When they departed, they drove up the Outer Drive toward the Loop. On the corner of State and Madison, Steinberg'd looked at him and grinned. The sidewalks were clogged with shoppers, it was a gorgeous autumn day. Where to, Stringer? Bring out the charts and set a course. What's the destination? Give me a route number.

Happy, Stringer laughed.

"North, south, where?"

"Anywhere," Stringer said. And Steinberg had put the car in gear and kept moving in the direction they were headed.

Stringer shook his head, clearing it of the past, and returned to the job at hand. Twenty yards from the road now, he took the black box out of his shirt and laid it under a bush. He concealed it beneath leaves and grass, then moved away. Now he was obliged to run parallel to the road for a mile or more, plant the second box, and return to the laager, where Price was. His mind was clear now, and his movement acquired a rhythm. One foot in front of the other, a dip of the shoulders, the pistol in his fist close to his body. Eyes up and watchful, head swiveling left and right, he did a slow dance through the forest, pausing every few steps on the off-beat. A hypnotic movement in its way, the dark green of the forest converging before his eyes; the look of the forest seductive and vibrant, feral, murderous, lonely.

Dawn. Exhausted, all attempt at concealment abandoned, Stringer made his way back up the mountain. He was shaking with fatigue, and parched. He knew he was safe, he'd eluded them. Both boxes were on the ground now, and there were no spares. He would never have to make the trip again. Fifty yards below the summit he became cautious again, moving more slowly. Bone weary, he knew there was no harmony and rhythm now. Harmony to hell. There was just one man stumbling ahead, shirt and trousers soaked with sweat and dew from the leaves. He paused when he reached the height and cautiously poked his head up, looking for Price.

He saw them both right away, eyes open and staring; both drenched with Price's blood. Stringer backed away, his eyes fastened on Price's face. Then his instinct asserted itself, and he scuttled back down the hill and crept off the path to make another approach. He slipped and fell twice, hanging on to trees and large rocks; the hill fell steeply away off the path. His mind raced: if there were one, there might be two. He believed there was only one (he'd seen him six hours before), but there was no way to be sure. He knew for certain that the two on the hill were dead.

Presently he poked his head up over the ridge at a point fifty yards away, and the scene was the same, undisturbed. The two men locked together, Price held by a knife's blade in the gut; the other by Price's fingers around his throat. They were not touching at any other point, they might have been politely approaching one another, preparing to shake hands. Except for the terrible expressions, the looks of shock and pain and rage; lost looks. The other one was smaller by five or six inches, he looked no older than a boy. But appearances were always deceptive. Stringer swept the ground with his eyes, then he walked over to the two dead men. He heard his own feet scrape the dirt and felt the breeze on his face. It was odd, but one had to look very closely to discern nationalities. Both men were dressed in black, both had blackened hands and faces. Price was hairier, that was the major difference; that and his height and his bone-white teeth. Stringer picked up the empty bottle of paregoric.

"Sick, I suppose," he muttered, and then his face crumbled as he looked again at the two men. He saw their expressions, and the film that had collected over the lenses of their eyes. The blood had turned dark and viscous.

The bodies were already stiff. Price's foot, an inch off the earth, hung suspended. Stringer went to his canteen and poured a cup of water and stood drinking, looking at the corpses. The water cooled him, cut a wet path down his throat to his stomach. It was then that he noticed the black vultures, three of them, drifting overhead in lazy circles. Any fool knew what that meant, and as soon as it was fully light there would be a patrol on the doorstep. The birds never moved their wings, except to make small lateral corrections; they coasted on wind currents. He looked at the birds and knew he would have to leave then, carrying the radio as well as his own pack. No point to bury the dead, it would take too much time. He'd leave with three canteens of water, his rifle, and as much ammunition as he could carry. The morphine, the small pack, and the bloody radio, twenty pounds of heavy metal; awkward to lift and impossible to conceal.

He thought briefly of Price, and of Price's last moments. Painful as hell, he said aloud. He thought about pain rather than fear. He retraced the route with his eyes, he imagined the smaller man crawling over the lip of the ridge, lying frozen for a moment, then in a swift fluid rush hitting Price in an instant. Price would have been asleep or dozing, which was worse than sleep because you thought you were awake. But he gave thanks that Price was dozing, not sleeping, and had excellent reflexes.

Stringer should have killed him on the mountain. He'd had the chance, though it was dangerous. Price had no chance at all. No one should have to die like that.

"It's all the same," Stringer said aloud.

The hell it is.

"No. That's the sad part about it. It truly is all the same."

Stringer stood very quietly and listened for a moment. It would take them two hours to move up the trail, because they'd be careful about it. They'd know that something was wrong, and in pursuit they'd be careful not to compound errors. Stringer thought that he would talk with Command, then leave. He could be on the move and off the mountain before the first enemy reconnaissance arrived. He quickly strung the antennae and switched on the radio.

"Dance Two this is Dance One. Are you reading?"

"One this is Dance Two. Proceed." They'd answered in a split second.

He wanted to tell them that Price was dead and he was evacuating the laager. There was no need to go into all the details. "Killed" would do it. He wanted to give them the new coordinates and suggest that they plan to pick him up on the following day. He had his map in front of him and was studying it. He'd move to a place no one ever heard of, where he'd be entirely safe. He coded all of this in his head.

"This is Dance One. Message commences." He waited five seconds, then spoke very clearly and slowly:

> "73498 22304 49487 10903 80372 90334
> 89340 59483 89356 00394 46831 13693
> 93847 24609 77373 22395 99301 19234
> 67843 96059 32973 39467 22564 09237

Message ends."

"One this is Two. Message received. Please repeat third group."

This was a code of another kind. He was meant to reverse the last two numerals. This was cute nonsense, on odd days of the month it meant reverse the first two numerals. Stringer said very slowly: "I am repeating third group. Four-niner-four-seven-eight. I repeat that. Four-niner-four-seven-eight."

"We have it," Command said.

" 'Bye," Stringer said, knowing that would irritate them. They hated any departure from procedure. But they had all the information now, and the mission was ended. Over. Done with. Finished. He could clear out. For this run they could do their own spotting. But God he was tired. He wished now he'd taken some of the pills they'd offered him. But he hated pills, all but the morphine, which was a different category of pill. You used morphine for pain, not for fatigue. He could rest for a few hours after he was free of the mountain. He could conceal himself in the forest and sleep for six hours, then move at high noon. Fine time for marching.

He patted Price's pockets to make certain that he had no personal identification of any kind. They were supposed to be pristine, the radio was Swedish, the weapons Czech, the boots Spanish, the scopes German, the wristwatches Japanese. Price was entirely clean, there was only a Swiss knife and a nondescript ballpoint pen. Stringer pitched Price's weapon down the slope. Then he dismantled the radio and put it in its pack and hoisted the pack to his back. He strapped three canteens around his waist and filled his pockets with ammunition. He had the morphine and the two bars of chocolate, the poncho and the paperback book in the small pack.

Well, he would give it a minute.

Stringer sat down again and lit a cigarette, watching the smoke blow away, smelling the good tobacco, feeling the smoke go deep into his lungs. It was a foolish risk to take, you could smell cigarette smoke a thousand meters away. But his luck had been so good, he figured he'd chance it. Luck was with him, nothing else mattered. He was alive and Price was dead. Stringer looked on Price with new respect: Price had done the very difficult, he'd completed the hardest problem. The war would be won or lost or ended, another hundred or another thousand would be killed. One, two more bombing runs that day; a thousand more until the war expired. Nothing would change. The war simply persisted, as a tree grew. As the war matured, it became cunning and artful; wise with age, it learned to endure and prevail, renewing itself at intervals, growing gnarled and stubborn with the years. Admired for its grandeur and virility, its broad-shouldered branches reached from an undying trunk. But nothing changed, except some souls lived and others died. The tree was indifferent to the people. It was a matter of chance, hazard. Stringer was now at the center of events.

But luck was with him. He sat with his back to the large rock, in the place where the radio had been. The two dead men lay embraced nearby. Stringer smoked a cigarette and thought about his good luck.

five

WITH A last look at the two dead, Stringer moved off the summit of the mountain. He'd removed every trace of the encampment, except of course for Price. There was no reason to think that Price was one of two. The lieutenant colonel commanding would look at Price and guess that he was a single spotter. Assuming that the lieutenant colonel commanding thought anything at all; with luck he and his troops would die in the raid. Stringer made haste, hurrying off the mountain; no one would guess his fatigue.

His movements were now a matter of rote, rhythm. He swung down the slope of the mountain on a lateral, turning from time to time, looking for any sign of life. His plan was very clear in his head, and it repeated itself inside his brain. He intended to move twenty miles to the east and radio then for a pickup. Easy as pie. He'd arrive at noon the following day, and be aboard ship by midafternoon. First the after-action report, then a drink and sleep. Then a holiday. Command would want to know every detail, particularly the circumstances of Price's killing. He'd give them a heroic tale, not far at all from the truth. Colonel Price would like that. And it would satisfy Command.

He and Steinberg were skilled at reporting. How many times had they done it? Four, five times perhaps. It was a detail apart from the war itself. Stringer participated in the war and allowed others to think about it; in that way, the war was exactly like life itself. One maneuvered inside the details, there was no possibility of making sense of the whole. The thing simply *was.* He was an accomplice to it in the same way that he was an accomplice to life. He'd happened to fetch up on the shores of a war, rather than some other shore. Not much rhyme nor reason to that. In the beginning they'd been required to hear lectures on the roots and purposes of the war. Military historians reached back into history for certain . . . metaphors. But the war had gone on for so long that these sounded like excursions into another century. And of course they were frantic to prove themselves correct. These were lectures punctuated with *if* at every turn. And there were so many turnings. Stringer and his friends squirmed: the historical section was becoming very important, it had its own compound at headquarters with a bar, a library, and a Xerox machine. "Documents in American Foreign Policy." A historian was more valuable than a high-ranking prisoner. The section was commanded by a brigadier general with a master's degree in Slavic studies and accountable only to COMUS himself. The historical section fit the bits and pieces of the war into a plausible whole. They had a grasp on all the after-action reports.

Wonderful. Stringer plunged forward, the radio pressing down on his back, his back muscles aching with the strain of it. One of the historians would be very useful now, he could use some grasp to lighten the fucking load. What kind of army was it that had a historical section editing the present for the benefit of the future? This was a historical section festooned with advanced degrees, scholars steeped in Great Books; they wrote essays on the Gothic progress of the war. Stringer wondered where the planes were, it would be a hell of a note if at the last minute they scrubbed the strike. They'd done that before, for reasons of their own. The green of the forest had a hypnotic effect on him, and he had to repeatedly check his compass; odd, because Stringer had an excellent sense of direction.

Stringer knew where he was, even inside the machine. If you went inside it, you had no choice but to serve it or sabotage it. If the choice were sabotage, then you had to accept the consequences. And it was dangerous! Stringer had no wish to live as a saboteur, it did not fit in with his plans. So he joined SAG instead, with an assist from the times and from tough-minded Steinberg. It might as easily have been General Motors, but of course was not. However, a case could be made that the machines and the men who ran them were identical. In any case, Washington seemed a safe haven for a few years; how could a man go entirely wrong working for the United States Government? With its guarantees of liberty and anonymity.

Command told him he had an enviable detachment, he wished he could bottle it and feed it to his other men. A morale builder. He wished Stringer's objectivity were a virus that was contagious, like flu.

— We could use more like you.

— You'll find them.

— It's more difficult than you think. You've no appreciation of the problems. We wash out nine of every ten applicants. That's a ninety percent failure. Ninety percent of the government's investment goes for naught, and it's a very expensive program. Try defending it to the accountants! I dare not tell you how expensive it is. And no one lasts a year.

— Don't count on me.

— We're not.

— I'm out after twelve months.

— That's the contract. We always honor the contract. No one's ever accused us of welching.

— Well, don't forget it.

— You've done a really excellent job, Stringer. I mean really *superb*. You've saved lives and your name is known. Outstanding. You've been careful. You'll have no trouble with another life, a new job, after you leave here. I'll give you a list of companies, you'll have first dibs. And top-class recommendations, I can promise that. You've saved lives and you've shortened the war.

— That's one way of looking at it.

— Stringer, it's the only way.

— One question?

The interview was friendly, and Stringer thought he would probe gently. He wanted to ask about Fowler, the officer alleged to've gone over the hill. Scandalous rumor surrounded Fowler. He watched Command's eyes narrow, and his fingers begin to tap on the desk top.

— I can't stop you from asking a question.

— What happened to Fowler?

— As you very well know, according to the procedures that we are bound to follow, Fowler is missing and presumed dead. There was an inquiry, we know nothing beyond that. All the rumor —

— Steinberg told me a little about the case.

— Steinberg talked too much, and his facts were not always straight.

— Still, there were suspicions. A presumption —

— What would be your guess, Stringer? Or better yet, what was Steinberg's guess. What did he have to say about the case? Fowler, a difficult and guarded man. Not altogether . . . there. A puzzle, that one. I can tell you this much. The inquiry was not a success.

— Inconclusive?

— Scrupulous, but not decisive.

— Steinberg was suspicious, but he had no theories.

— That was good of him.

— Would you say he's alive?

— Fowler? I shouldn't be surprised, although there is no way of knowing. And I can tell you this. We've tried.

— Wasn't he one of your best? That was my understanding. Wasn't he a man of the future?

— I think Fowler did not understand the rules. In any case, he's lost to us now.

The interview ended and Stringer left Command's office for the O Club bar. It was one thing they didn't stint on, the liquor was the very best — Scotch whiskey, English gin, German beer, French Pernod, and Fitzhugh rattling the liars' dice cup, perched on a stool in a corner of the room. Oh Stringer, Fitzhugh cried when he learned of the interview. The compliments, the promise of a job, the assurance that references would be supplied. Lucky devil, Fitzhugh said. "They like you, Stringer. You're in like Flynn."

Cynical Fitz knew nothing of Fowler.

He slapped at a red ant on his arm and then jumped as he felt the bombs and heard the roar. The fresh sensors had done their work, the ground thumped as if struck by giant drumsticks. Then came the low tremulous roar, after the earth had stilled. It was impossible to tell, but Stringer thought they were off target; too far to the south. But it made no difference now, the bombs gave him confidence. He was off and running, in five hours' time he could rest. He was dangerously tired now, but he could not stop. He'd already laid one false trail, and doubled back on it. He did not believe they were good trackers, but he wanted to take every precaution. The radio was deadweight on his back, and the ammunition weighed his pockets down; the rifle was a necessary nuisance, awkward in his fist. But he was in good spirits after the bombing, almost cheerful, encouraged by the explosions over the mountain. He knew that he was on his way now, and there was nothing they could do to prevent him. He tried to forget about the weight on his back and the fatigue, the ants and the heat and the sweat that slicked his face and body.

Stringer walked on until noontime, picking his way blindly through a high forest crisscrossed by natural pathways. The forest floor was soft, and heavy with moss. Stringer saw no evidence of habitation, nor any animal life except for gray birds cruising overhead. The birds followed him like the pilot fish of a shark.

At exactly twelve noon he shucked his pack and the radio and placed them under cover of a small bush. The land undulated now, and he found himself on the side of a small hill with a commanding view of the countryside. But he was well concealed. He took the chocolate and the paperback out of his pack and rested against a pine tree. His feet ached, and a blister was coming up on his left heel. Stringer slowly extracted a cigarette, lit it, and leaned back. He watched his hands tremble. No more of this, he thought. This was the last *one*, the last of the line. He was too old to be this tired. He sipped from a cup of water and chewed the chocolate and felt better. The heat was not bad. He'd survive all right. He felt some of the tension leave him. The rifle needed cleaning, so he very slowly took it apart and cleaned the barrel and the breech. Then he oiled the moving parts and checked that the clip was full. It was an excellent weapon so long as it was kept clean, meaning spotless. Dirty, the action had a tendency to jam.

The chocolate tasted good on his tongue. He took another sip of water and replaced the canteen. Not much for a meal, but all he had. Well, it was enough. He tried to think of the water as wine, a rich Burgundy from Beaune. Competing flavors, the texture of the wine on his tongue. He smiled. No imagination could do that. This wine was water, flavored with halizone. It tasted rancid. It slaked his thirst, nothing more. He felt nicely tired now and put away the water and the chocolate. He made a pillow of his pack and pushed in further into the bush. He was utterly alone, but he went through the motions of camouflage. He lay on his side, the rifle barrel near his right eye. His hand was gripped around the trigger guard, the safety was off. He thought about his after-action report to Command. What Command would say. He wondered about the second raid and decided he was wrong about the planes being off course. Certainly they were on course. The coordinates were absolutely clear and accurate, and the sensors were well placed. But the hell with it. That was their problem. He was done with it. He'd done his job, he'd fulfilled the contract and now he could get away. He had enough money for five years. Perhaps he'd go back to New Hampshire and ski. Or to Europe. That seemed improbable, it was so far away. It took a leap of the imagination to think of it at all, like trying to believe the water was wine. He could not see himself in a ski lodge in New Hampshire. That would never happen, he had to put it out of his mind. Get out of here first, then think of the future. It was useless thinking of the future right now. He tentatively tried to imagine the White Mountains, the lodge near Hanover. It was like picking his way through a minefield, he did not want to imagine too much. But he thought of the hills, sharp and lovely, not indistinct as the hills he saw now. Light, not dark; white, not green; cold, not heat. Lovely various whites, rolling to a jagged horizon. He pulled himself back, tugging his mind into the present. Sleep, then a pickup. They could pick him up at noon the next day, he had only twenty-four hours to wait. That was not long. He closed his eyes and thought about time, in minutes and in hours, and then in distance. He was too tired to fall asleep. His eyes kept popping open, and he closed them with difficulty. Everything was soft and silent, the sun filtering greenly through the trees. He thought briefly about the old cabin in New Hampshire, and then about his wife; wherever she was now. They'd had a hell of a time. Sleep was elusive, fighting him. Presently he felt himself slipping. Then he was asleep.

He came to consciousness slowly, knowing right away that something was wrong. He kept his eyes closed and as he came awake he tried to use his other senses. His hearing told him nothing, the place was silent as a tomb. Something was wrong with his sense of touch, and he did not understand what it was. He moved his hands very slowly over the trigger guard of his rifle. His fingers were touching each other. No trigger guard, no rifle, and the smell of someone else near him; the odor was strong and sour. He mumbled something guttural and indistinct, wanting the other to believe he was still asleep. But the hairs on the back of his neck were beginning to rise, and he felt himself starting to tremble. The trembling was internal, it would not be noticed. Just then he was turned over by a hard kick in the ribs, and his eyes jumped open. He slowly put his hands out to show that he was unarmed; then he turned his head to see who it was.

"American?"

Stringer nodded.

"Be still."

Stringer obeyed.

"Pilot?"

Stringer shook his head.

"Imperialist spy?"

Stringer shrugged.

"Turn around again. Keep your eyes on the ground."

Stringer squinted his puzzled look, as if he didn't understand, and the other motioned for him to turn away, to lie as he had been. He did not know whether it would be an advantage to admit that he knew the language. He ought to conceal what advantages he had, there were not many in sight. Language would mark him as a dangerous American. He heard the radio being unpacked and tinkered with, and his knapsack opened. Every couple of seconds, he felt the barrel of the rifle between his shoulder blades. He'd only had a moment to look at his captor, and he'd not been reassured: an impassive dark face with a long scar running down one cheek. Pitch-black eyes and stringy hair, the body dressed in black. He could only be military, there was no one else in the area. Except that was what he'd thought on the road too, and there'd been the two old men, the ones he called Laurel and Chaplin and then killed. This one held the rifle with security, he was no stranger to weapons. His leg was developing a cramp now, and when he tried to straighten it the rifle barrel was hard into his back and the voice barked a command. Stringer thought it was useless concealing anything then and said slowly, pain in his voice: "The leg is injured. And there's a cramp. I want to straighten it. I'm unarmed and" — he groped a moment for the correct word — "harmless."

"Be still," the other said.

"Screw you," Stringer said in English, very pleasantly. The way he said them, they were words of agreement.

He lay closer to the earth, the leg hurting. The cramp began in his thigh and was stabbing into the hip. It would be useful if he could lead the other to believe that the leg was seriously damaged in some way.

"Sit up."

Stringer sighed and sat up, rubbing his eyes. He was careful to move with deliberation. He sat with his back to a tree, rubbing his leg and scowling. The other was ten yards away, sitting cross-legged in the soft soil. His expression was bland.

"You know the language well." Stringer nodded, disconcerted. "Where did you learn it?"

"The Americans have language schools," Stringer said carefully. "I went to one in the state of California. They have special techniques, and it's possible to learn the language in a year. I was good, and at the end of the year I was fluent. A Class One, according to their reckoning."

"Where are you based?"

Stringer told him, volunteering the name of his unit as well.

"And your mission?"

131

"A man named Price and I were sent as spotters for convoys. We had electrical equipment that guided the aircraft. We used that radio" — Stringer nodded at the pack — "to contact our Command."

"You were responsible for the raid yesterday?"

"I was."

"It must be very easy."

"I suppose it is," Stringer said. "Easy but expensive. These are very expensive air raids."

"Americans do not lack money."

This was all said in a low singsong, smooth and slow and quiet. The other sat perfectly still, nodding, as if his last remark said all that needed to be said.

"You will be pleased to know that it was a successful raid."

Stringer nodded noncommittally.

"A very successful raid, and you are technically a spy, and as such can be shot."

Stringer nodded. "Correct."

"Where is your comrade?"

"Dead. One of your people killed him."

"And how was that done?"

"Last night one of your soldiers came to our camp with a knife. Price was asleep or not alert. One or the other. He was attacked, but managed to strangle his attacker. I found them both this morning, and then left our camp. I thought I was clear." Stringer smiled. "You surprised me."

"The guiding. How is it done?"

Stringer explained about the sensors, their shape and what they did. The radio, the antennae, the computers at headquarters, the other details. His language was not equal to technical jargon, so his answer was slow and awkwardly phrased. His captor shook his head wearily, as if it were all too much to comprehend. Too intricate, too sophisticated for such a simple problem.

"What is your name?"

Stringer thought a moment, confused. "It won't translate," he said finally. "I can give you the American for it. The English."

"Do."

"Stringer."

"Your rank?"

"I have no rank. I have a courtesy title of major or colonel, depending on the circumstances. But for these circumstances, I have no rank. For a soldier like yourself, Mr. Stringer."

"An honorific?"

"Something like that," Stringer said. "Do you mind if I have a drink of water?"

"Later."

Stringer sat impassively, waiting for the next question.

"How long have you been in my country?"

"Eight days? Seven days, perhaps."

"And you planned to stay how long?"

"A week longer." Stringer suppressed a smile, the question sounded like a travel agent's. Or a customs official.

"What was your friend's rank?"

"Captain."

"So you outranked him."

"Sometimes I did, sometimes I didn't. It depended on the situation. Where we were and what we were doing.

The nature of the decision. In some cases I deferred to him. Others not."

Stringer was watching his man carefully, surprised at the moderate language. He could not fix an exact age, but guessed forty or forty-five, perhaps more. Except for the rifle, this might be a conversation between friends. He'd decided to hold nothing back; the longer he could keep the man talking the more chance there was for a stray strand of luck. That was all he could count on now, luck. He was surprised he was alive, every minute was in that way a gift. His captor showed no signs of killing him.

"May I know your name and rank?"

The other shrugged, imitating Stringer.

"You're military?"

"In my country, we are all military. One unit or another. The correct way in my country is the military way." A flicker of a smile. "The correct way in this case being the only way."

"Your camp is nearby?"

"If this language is too tiring for you, we can speak French."

A signal, Stringer thought. "No, my French is very bad."

"I have a little English. But I prefer French."

"Your choice."

"I prefer my own language to either English or French."

"*D'accord,*" Stringer said.

The man with the rifle was silent for a moment. Then: "What do you think of our military leadership?"

"I try to think about it as little as possible," Stringer replied, curious if his man would understand the play.

"Say that again?" He didn't.

"I don't think about it. It has very little to do with me." Stringer gambled: "I'm the puppet at the end of a string —"

"Now you're lying," the other said. "You've been telling the truth, but now you're lying. You lied just then, you do not think of yourself as a puppet. Far from it. That is not your role inside or out, in this life or the next. Why did you lie? I don't like lies."

"Apologies. But your leadership really does not concern me. I suppose it is adequate for what it does. More than adequate. There are those who say it is brilliant, truly innovative. They say your leadership has rewritten the handbook on infantry tactics. No small achievement, if the experts are correct."

He waited a long time before replying, measuring Stringer with his eyes. His look was opaque, his eyes hard and dark. There was no movement in his expression. He started to say something, then apparently thought better of it. The gun barrel did not waver. Stringer grew nervous under his stare and asked again for water. Request refused.

"A cigarette, then?"

"Later."

Stringer waited, conscious of the failing light; he moved his legs, massaging them with both hands.

"What concerns you then, spy? What is on your conscience? Your life, your comfort? Your wife, perhaps, some second self? What is it? You can let me in on the secret, if that is what it is."

Perplexed, Stringer said nothing.

"The leadership does not concern you, your own acts do not concern you. What does?" He shifted the rifle so that it pointed at Stringer's chest.

"Stay alert, stay alive," Stringer said.

"Just so."

"Slogans," he said with a smile.

"I would have to call you a very modern man."

"Ahead of my time?"

"Yours and mine."

"The difference between revolution and reaction," Stringer said. He couldn't tell where the conversation was going. He was following it, wherever it was going.

"You are like a brick in a wall, very difficult to dislodge. And you face in both directions. Perhaps you cannot be dislodged at all. Perhaps that is the point. You are in the center of the compass." The voice sounded faint to Stringer. "But you are well indoctrinated, no doubt of that."

He had lapsed into French, and Stringer did not get all of it. He leaned forward, and his captor repeated the phrase in his own language. Stringer waited a moment before replying.

"What is the incidence of insanity in your country?" he asked at last.

"Insanity? In the small towns and villages, quite high. It is a thing from birth, usually. If a child can reach the age of eight or nine the chances are excellent that he will survive and remain sane. There is another crisis point at thirty-five or forty, that is what the doctors tell us. That is the second climax, and the most dangerous. But of course the doctors are sometimes wrong."

"What do you do with your crazies?"

The other one smiled, as if he were about to make a joke. But when he spoke, he was serious. "They are cared for at home, most of them. Unless they are violent, in which case they are taken to institutions and cared for there. It is a disgrace to be taken to an institution, no family wants to do that with one of its own. It is a form of surrender, and is officially discouraged. We stress self-help."

"Self-help, is it?"

"So they say."

"But you don't believe it?"

"I believe self-help has its limits."

"I suppose your definitions are similar to ours?"

"I'd guess so."

Stringer leaned forward, translating slowly. "Schizophrenia. Mania. Depression. Paranoia. Hallucinations. Fits of weeping. Indescribable sorrow. Guilt. Loss."

"One would imagine."

"Violent outbursts?"

"But of course."

"It's good to know that these conditions are universal."

"Two countries are not the universe, spy."

Stringer nodded, a reasonable correction. "Perhaps I could have the cigarette now."

"Throw the package to me."

Stringer dug into his shirt pocket and tossed the package of Camels. His captor, the enemy, took two cigarettes from it, lit them both, and threw one back to Stringer. He flipped it underhand, and the cigarette bounced off Stringer's shoe in a little shower of sparks.

"You'll be interested to know. The aircraft, yours, destroyed a battalion of men, one of our most experienced units, by the way, and eight tanks all told. Some trucks, one or two ammunition carriers. And a field hospital. It was remarkably efficient. Incredible, really — and this was a unit that had been together for many years, from the time of the creation of the war. Its fighting record was a source of inspiration. The commanding officer was an old friend, we were born in the same district and it was said that we were distantly related. He was a brave man, many times decorated in the field. There are only a few such men in any army, and I grieve now for his life. Without warning the planes struck and five hundred men were killed or so seriously wounded as to be as good as dead. A number were knocked senseless, and I mean that literally. They are now without sense, their heads empty. Anything can now enter the head, all defenses have been broken down; these men are no longer alive, they are merely living. They flit about like butterflies. The concussion and the shock, the blast. They are the ones who are as good as dead. Worse, perhaps. You've seen them?"

"I've seen our own in that condition," Stringer said. "Yesterday I saw yours from a distance. It's not necessary to be up close."

"You were pleased?"

"The job was done. I know what bombing does to . . .

troops. I wasn't pleased, far from it. But it was remote, you understand?" Stringer looked into blank eyes. "There was a terrible beauty about it, you'd understand that." He paused again. "But it becomes impersonal."

"Yes."

Dusk came on them, the long shadows lengthening.

"That must be admitted. One must admit that to understand the other." Stringer smiled. "It isn't any aberration."

"One is not proud."

"No."

The shadows fell across both faces, obscuring them. Stringer shifted position, but the other did not move. For a moment, Stringer wondered if he were asleep. The other was camouflaged, his legs looked like two black branches, akimbo in the grass; as night fell, his features blended into the vegetation. The voice was entirely disembodied now. It was confusing. Stringer squinted into the middle distance.

"When will the helicopter come?"

"When I tell it to come." Stringer pointed at the radio.

"And when will that be?"

"Tomorrow afternoon sometime."

"And will it come? Like that? On a signal from you?"

"That's the plan."

"How long have you been . . . doing this?"

"Three, four years. On and off. One assignment or another. Here and there. And you?"

"More than that." Smiling. "A long time, many years."

"Too long," Stringer said, in sympathy. They were two

old soldiers, comrades-in-arms. They had much in common, their experiences were similar. Soldiers were the same the world over, like artists or businessmen. "No," his enemy said. "Not necessarily. I don't know what 'too long' means. It's as long as it is necessary to be. Perhaps it is forever, I mean for one's lifetime. Not encouraging, but likely. No evidence to the contrary, one looks for evidence but it is difficult to find. But we are not weary. To become weary of this war is to become weary of life." He paused, there was a stifling silence. "We are not a nation of suicides. It is not in the national tradition, for better or worse." The voice, so even and humdrum, lulled Stringer; he yawned and settled back against the tree. His cigarette had gone out, but he did not notice that.

"You and I . . ." Stringer began.

". . . we understand," his enemy said, and laughed harshly. A blast of laughter, dissipating in the dark.

Stringer's hands were flat against the damp earth, palms down. He listened intently, but the voice did not speak again. It was entirely dark now, and Stringer could see nothing. His eyelids began to close, he fought against sleep. He realized he was frightened, he did not want to be alone in the dark. Even an enemy was preferable to that. He listened to the night sounds, a soft rustle in the trees and the grass. He forced a lightness into his voice, speaking in deliberate English. "What's the program, Comrade? What are your plans? Do you have an itinerary?"

There was no answer.

"Are you there?"

Silence.

". . . an imperialist spy in your midst. An international war criminal, destroyer of a battalion." He listened, bent forward. "A counterrevolutionary, something vital. Evil."

Stringer was hot and sweating. He tried to lift his arms but could not. He felt himself falling backward, unbalanced. In panic, he fought against it. His mind clouded, and he began to fall very slowly. Tumbling in slow motion. He was forced to let go entirely then, and he fell asleep.

Dawn, cold and gray. A light rain fell through the trees, so fine as to be almost a mist. The land was covered with haze, the terrain blurred and ghostly. Stringer had slept through the night, unaware, in the middle of a strange dream. He dreamed he was being held captive in a nearly airless room, a room without furniture or windows; he was being made to stand at attention in the center of the room, away from the white walls. There were no lamps, but the room was light, bright as day. When he woke he was terribly thirsty and his head hurt, and he was alone. The rifle was stuck to his clammy fists, loaded, off safety. The canteens were nearby. The radio was wrapped in its canvas cover, undisturbed.

A hallucination. It happened often, common to men who are alone for long periods "in uncertain circumstances," ships' captains or solitary soldiers. When Slocum sailed alone around the world he was befooled, imagining that the skipper of the *Pinta* took his sloop through a storm in the North Atlantic. Slocum and the phantom skipper conversed, and the ship held its course though

Slocum was ill below decks. From his bunk he watched the ghost steer his boat, the extraordinary and durable *Spray*. Hallucinations were common to ships' captains and soldiers, one reason why the testimony of both was unreliable. Eyes and brains were not equal to the circumstances, they were too selective. Soldiers and ships' captains, no one took their evidence seriously, there were contradictions and outright lies. Fabrications, fantasies, embroideries on events. These were men who could not distinguish between what they saw and heard and what they felt. With the necessary transpositions, fact and fiction merged and became one.

Stringer smiled sourly. Perhaps his time was now. Up. Like Boone. Like (he supposed) Steinberg, wherever Steinberg was now, in whatever direction Steinberg was headed.

Wearily, he gathered up his equipment. The pack, the radio, the rifle, his canteens. His watch said a quarter after six, there was no way to check it by the angle of the sun or the look of the shadows. Stringer brushed the water off his face and took a drink from his canteen. It was all well and good to know about hallucinations and their random nature. But it was the first time it had happened to him, and it was nothing to be happy about or pleased with. He stared at the compass in his hand.

The world looked strange to him. The green was replaced by gray, the lowering clouds covered the earth with a fine mist, gray water. The land was bleak and gently rolling. He'd roll with it, become part of its contour and thereby invisible to his enemies. But he had to concentrate now, particularly on the set of his compass.

Stringer mostly depended on dead reckoning, and what he considered an intuitive sense of direction. But the mist obscured the land and there was no seeing the way out. He was in trouble if he could not estimate the co-ordinates on his map. He could roll with the earth all right, and end up under it if he wasn't careful. He'd withdrawn about as far into himself as it was possible to go, that being the only sure way of survival; in an inhuman situation, one strived to shut down all the unnecessary engines. What was it his friend the enemy said? You are like a brick in a wall, faced in both directions. Become part of the earth, Stringer told himself; the earth friendly. In that spirit, Stringer pressed east — walking carefully but quickly, mindful that the area was supposed to be deserted, but that it was quite possibly not; quite possibly there were patrols from elsewhere. It seemed to him that he was walking into his future, with no guideposts or landmarks to verify his position.

Enemies all around him, Stringer walked steadily for three hours, through the underbrush and the red ants, through mist so thick that the world dissolved into gray a few feet ahead of his eyes. At ten in the morning he halted for a drink of water and a reconsideration. He thought there was no reason to go farther. The mountain was behind him now, he was walking through empty terrain. They could pick him up here as well as there. He'd gone far enough, as far as he was able; he'd reached the end of the line. Stringer groped for the radio, unwrapped it, and strung the antennae.

"Dance Two this is Dance One. Are you reading?"

He pushed the switch and listened to the static of the

radio. When there was no answer, he routinely adjusted the dial.

"Dance Two this is Dance One. Are you reading me?"

It had never taken them more than a second and a half. But now there was silence. The pricks, Stringer thought; a nation of inattentive pricks.

"Dance Two this is Dance One. Serious. Urgent."

Stringer pushed the switch and adjusted the antennae. The static grew, but there was no response.

"Dance Two, Dance Two. White Wing." That was a special signal for someone in trouble, *beaucoup* trouble as Command liked to define it; anyone within hearing distance was obliged to come in on the net.

As before, there was silence.

"Dance Two this is Dance One. White —"

"Dance One this is Dance Two." The signal was faint, but it was there. An unfamiliar voice.

"Where the fuck were you?"

"In code, please."

"Fuck the code! Where —"

"*Code!*"

Stringer was trembling with anger. The pricks. Oh the pricks, some shavetail in the communications tent playing God with his code book, wanting to hear the *numbers*. Well, there was nothing else to do. He would ask them in code, where the fuck were you?

"Dance Two this is Dance One. Message commences:

49380 90294 87363 44870 19230 87909
79823 89023 65872 11589 24353 44562."

144

And the beauty of that was that if the others were listening in they could break the code. They'd have the key to it, if they could break down "fuck." It depended on their command of the vernacular. Because the wonder of the code was its simplicity; it was very easy to commit to memory, to encode and decode, once you'd studied it for a day or two. Simple, and very difficult to break (according to the computers; it had taken the most sophisticated computers they had one month to break the code). Five men working part-time had been at it for a year without success, and they were competent men. But the computer was more sophisticated. So Command would be angry, and with reason.

Stringer smiled as the reply fluttered back, a bit quicker than usual.

"One this is Two. Message commences.

93847	17875	23091	35561	84483	45591
19267	23645	09823	39486	54298	27569
11096	83456	12398	00687	18905	97850
07936	13459	30905	70039	99956	00001
38475	19365	21393	65923	36489	67973."

Yes, they were angry.

Now Stringer could get down to business. Where he would be picked up and when. The damned mist made it difficult, he could not be absolutely certain where he was. But the radio made dead reckoning unnecessary. Despite the damp and the chill, Stringer was sweating. The straps on his radio pack had marked the flesh on his back, and his shirt was soaked through. He sat down heavily now, to make the dizziness go away. He felt the stubble on his chin and jaw and sighed. Make it easy, he thought; move for one hour, perhaps two, and arrange pickup then.

An ant was on his neck, he felt it poking around. It bit, hard, and Stringer winced and slapped the back of his neck. Oh shit, the ants; he moved out from under the tree branch. The things were as big as spiders. He looked at his fingers and saw a blood smear. And from a few feet away, he heard a dry chuckle, like the rustle of old bones. His friend was back. His enemy, perched on the stump of a tree. Stringer could smell its flesh. He backed away, feeling the sweat run down the sides of his face. There were no words from it, only the dry chuckle and a wide smile. A mirthless grin, from ear to ear.

"You're not suited to this country. It's difficult enough for those of us who live here. For an intruder, it's impossible. I imagine that it's something to do with the climate. The humidity and the soil."

"What happened to you this morning?"

"I had to leave. But I'm back now."

"I thought you were a hallucination, or possibly only an illusion. A figment of my imagination."

He laughed: "No."

"Well, they're common enough."

"There was a question about what to do with you."

Stringer looked cautiously to one side, searching for the rifle.

"The disposition of the body."

He couldn't find it.

"To put your mind at rest."

Stringer bent his head into his knees. He did not want

146

to faint, but he felt himself slipping. He tried to remember where he was, the coordinate numbers. He was somewhere west of the river, perhaps five miles west; the river was west of the shore. He was traveling east, or trying to. That was where they were waiting for him. He'd accumulated too much, he thought. There was too much inside his head. Morphine wasn't worth a damn for what he had.

His enemy grinned at him, a loathsome little man in a black suit. There was nothing comfortable about him. He was still an animal at rest, with the same potential for movement; a poised little figure.

"You might as well sleep."

Stringer made no reply.

"I'll take the radio."

"No!"

"Yes, that's definite."

Stringer struggled to his feet, searching wildly for the rifle. He saw it propped against the radio, fully loaded, safety off. He reached it in two steps and quickly squeezed off one shot, then another. The gun jumped in his hand. He put the rifle on automatic and sprayed the trees. He emptied one clip, leaning against the radio; he bent forward with the rifle. Sobbing, he put it down. Of course his enemy had vanished and was no place to be seen now. Stringer'd known that and had aimed high; he'd aimed at the treetops, not wanting to harm anything. He wanted to protect himself without damaging anything else. Tears mingled with sweat and the fine rain, the mist that had plagued him since morning. A sad persistent mist, it covered the earth like the steam from a cauldron. Stringer doubled up again, his head between his knees; he tried to retch but could not, his empty stomach yielded nothing.

The idea was to create a pocket of disorder, or misrule. It was tightly enclosed, a piece of its own, a world apart, like a chessboard or a playing field. Nothing else was germane. Command saw the war in that way, "the only war available to us." Ways and means. The means were carefully stylized, but subject to revision and modification, improvisation. A musical theme, becoming ever more cacophonous. What began as a simple child's melody was now a crazy symphony, with every instrument in the orchestra horning in. Command disliked Stringer's war, a basic struggle of one on one. It could not be justified in that way. The other could be controlled by computers, no man could grasp its disparate elements and themes, its metaphors and scenarios. It was richly plotted and harmonized. Naval and air metaphors, ground metaphors; psychological, political, economic, social, geological; urban metaphors and agrarian metaphors, the world of the mountain and the world of the swamp. Theology and propaganda. All these strings wound back to Command, but he did not pull them; he did not control, he monitored.

Stringer thought of Price, dutiful Price. Promotion-list Price, the prize major. The captain breveted major, the body would now be stiff as a board and beginning to stink. Major Price was now a name on a long list, or would be when Stringer filed his report; they would wait for something in writing before informing the family. Until Stringer returned, Price was as good as alive! When

148

they read the report, they would fabricate date and place of death, inventing a battle somewhere, quite possibly a heroic stand. Lurid, in the manner of all war stories. It was altogether possible that Steinberg would be in charge of this citation, his editorial duties were heavy. Steinberg's trademark was the barely concealed redundancy, *Major Price at considerable risk to his own life threw himself on an enemy hand grenade and thereby perished. But his comrades survived, thanks to* . . . This was a letter cleanly typed and prepared in quintuplicate. No doubt there would also be a posthumous Silver Star, undiscovered back pay; and Steinberg would craft a personal message from Command, and perhaps even the civilian secretary. These documents were severely grammatical, *I write with a real sense of loss and sadness* . . .

Price died for your sins, Stringer thought. Or perhaps for his own, he was not alert and therefore not alive. No, Price did not die for anyone's sins. Price did not have a concept of human sin, poor Price. Price was just-a-man-doing-a-job, doing what he was paid to do. And doing it well! Doing it with competence and control, a battalion of troops and six — or was it seven? — light tanks destroyed. He'd engaged an enemy unit, as he'd been instructed to do.

Stringer's mind wandered and then slipped free. He felt himself unhinge and saw the colors of the earth change. He wanted to go home, but did not know where that was. He could not fix the city or the country, no house came to mind, no lawn or porch or person. No single room. Slumping, idle, feverish Stringer pawed the dials of the radio, no longer knowing what he was doing.

In another region of his mind he heard the satisfied hum and the slick static. He crouched before the radio, muttering. Tears slipped from his eyes and carved a path down his cheeks. Self-sufficient Stringer, a hard nut; a thick skin, a tough mind. He heard a voice in the middle distance.

". . . Two. Are you hearing?"

He looked up.

"This is Two. Urgent."

He felt he had to put the pieces together. They were scattered about.

"One this is . . ."

He shook his head to clear it.

". . . Two."

Trees bent toward him.

"Give us your position."

They leaned, old men's fingers reaching. The mist settled, grew denser. A heavy and dense gray, mixed with green. He had to keep his hold on the ground. But he grew faint, choking.

"We assume east of your former position. How many miles? Can you signal? You're to use the radio . . ."

He feigned sleep, as he did as a boy. If he convinced them that he was asleep, they'd go away. They always did, believing him dreaming, dead to the world. He tucked his head under his arm, adopting a peaceful expression; an expression of calm, a peaceful smile, the innocent look of an infant.

"One this is Command. We will stay on this net. We're scrambling now. You must hold. Understand that this is a max effort. Repeat max effort. Nothing spared. But you must signal in the usual way, repeat in the usual way. *Comprenez?* We will stay on this net. We're scrambling, but you must hold on. Understand that this is a max effort, nothing spared. But you must signal. The radio. In the usual way. One this is Command . . ."

They'd created the pocket of disorder, God alone knew how. It was as if they had to have that to contrast with the other. Mountains were defined by plains, order was defined by chaos; it would not exist in a vacuum, alone. But he wished he knew the rules. There were too many rules to keep straight; these were practical and theoretical rules, some learned by training, some learned by instinct. There were too many loose rules to keep straight. They discovered and disclosed some, and withheld others. That was the way it was done, at every level. It had a logic of its own, if a man could understand it.

". . . in thirty minutes. One."

His eyes snapped open.

"One this is Command."

His rifle was in his hands, cradled, off safety.

"In thirty minutes, plus or minus five. We have the general position, but you must signal repeat signal. This is a max effort, do you understand? The entire team's here, we're behind you. You must come in now with your position, the coordinates. Repeating message . . ."

Stringer drew himself up, standing beside the radio. He had to find cover, a place to tuck away. No luck, the mist was clearing. He rubbed his eyes, digging his palms into the sockets of his eyes. Then he turned to the rifle, dangling in his fist. Meticulously he checked the trigger, the sight, the breech, the barrel. He threw away the used clip and reloaded with a fresh one. He could see the tops of the trees now, the mist was dissipating, burned off by the sun. The pale fire of the sun shone through the gray air, revealing a small clearing, an empty box in the forest. If they came, he could see them. But he could not remember the signal. It was a word not a number, but the word eluded him. He would not need it anyway, he had no intention of answering the radio message. So they would come from the east: east traveling west, and very low. He would hear them before he'd see them. That had been the way in the past, although in the past he'd been able to supply them with coordinates. They were flying blind this time, clearly an advantage. An advantage to him, as Steinberg was fond of explaining. He'd worked out the theory from a variety of sources. *Members of an organization depend on authority and leadership. The problem is not to destroy either authority or leadership or their various functions. Nor eliminate them. No, that would destroy the organization itself. The real problem of our time is to make leadership and the exercise of authority operate according to the accepted values and beliefs of our society. So the authority must be reformed from within! To make the crime fit the punishment.*

That was the theory, according to Steinberg. But Steinberg had a way of juicing the story and hashing up the quotes. So it was impossible to be sure. You had to listen, really *listen,* to Steinberg when he was citing sources.

"One this is Command. Answer please."

Stringer smiled self-consciously.

"We are making max effort."

Radio talk, Stringer thought. It was like no other.

"Stay at your location. Repeat remain at your location."

The equipment was truly miraculous.

Stay put, the radio said; don't move a muscle. But remember to signal at the sound of engines. The signal could make the difference. If the coast was clear or not, was what they meant; they wanted Stringer to warn them if they were flying into an ambush. Stringer was their link with that, the only one they had.

"Stringer this is Command" — they were informal all of a sudden, chatty, conversational. "D'you hear? Repeating message. Stringer from Command. The signal, Stringer. Are you reading?"

No, he read nothing.

"Stringer, what a job you've done. We're proud. The second strike was right on the money. Stringer, do you hear? You should be proud. You're outstanding." This was a new voice, damp with emotion. Stringer smiled sadly.

Where were they now?

"You should've seen it, we sent in an aircraft to verify the damage. The second strike was as letter-perfect as the first! This is the greatest two days in the history of the war!" The radio fell silent, then Command spoke again.

"You've done a hell of a job, Stringer. You put out for us, now we're putting out for you. We're sparing nothing, that's why I'm *en clair*. But we must have your help, you understand that. *What's your situation?*" There was a pause. Then, more slowly: "You must signal your coordinates. Where you are. And the situation. *What is your exact location?*"

153

He heard the aircraft, helicopters. Two, he guessed; possibly three. They were south, to his right; he thought about half a mile. They were very close, someone had navigated well; someone's instructions were working overtime. The sound of the engines and the huge blades retreated and Stringer was left alone again. Command was talking to him, but he took no notice. The metallic accents spilled out and were gone. This would be his last trick, and he had to be scrupulous about it. No false starts, thought Stringer; no wasted motion. They were flying contour, easy to hit (he'd seen it happen two dozen times, and once he'd felt the shock and heard the explosion, become hypnotized by the look of fifty calibers, the shells big as golf balls and visible, wavering, undulating, hot and lethal). He'd aim for the engine: with engine failure, the power gone, the thing would drop like a stone and spin into the trees, and then it would be *message concluded* for keeps. They would not be expecting it, an attack would come as a surprise to them. If there were three ships, it was conceivable that he could destroy two; a fair enough average, a reasonable score. If there were two, he'd get one for sure. Stringer sat with his back to the tree, the gun butt in his stomach.

The sound returned, the bird to his left this time. There were definitely two, possibly three. Stringer realized he was sweating, his temples pounding. They were on the far side. He would have to be very accurate, his small-caliber gun often ricocheted. He might be better off with a .45 and its heavier slug, but he could not squeeze off the rounds fast enough. Not as fast or as accurately as the rifle, which he knew as a friend. The radio was silent and Stringer waited for the helicopters to make their next swing.

He heard the noise of the engines before he saw them, but he was ready. When the black nose of the chopper cleared the trees he homed in on it and burped the entire clip. He aimed at the machine itself, forgetting about accuracy or anything but the hit itself; the machine looked big as a truck, and he thought he could see the bullets strike and make their pattern front to back. He felt them in the nerves of his body, *thuckthuckthuckthuckthuck*. He saw the startled look on the face of the door gunner and saw too, or thought he saw, the cigarette drop from his mouth and whip away in the wind stream. He knew he'd hit them dead on, not a single wasted bullet. They were beyond him when he heard two useless bursts from the chopper's machine gun, and then an explosion. The first chopper had crashed and now Stringer was worried that the pilot had time to radio *Mayday Mayday Mayday*.

He was exhausted, his rifle lay pointed at his feet. It was empty, he had no strength or desire to reload. The stink of gunpowder was in his nostrils, empty cartridge cases littered the ground around him. He heard the second aircraft before he felt the jolt of the rockets in and around the clearing. Stringer did not move. He let the shells fall, let the clumps of earth and trees tumble around him. Blue smoke and dirt and shock, and the racket of explosions. This was not his affair, it was part of something else altogether; the effect of some other cause. But he'd paid them back, he'd administered his own punishment. He did not move but waited for death.

His friend, his enemy. They'd lay waste the entire zone, they wouldn't stop until they'd killed every living thing, plant or animal; that was their way, the way it was done. Stringer thought about that, curled up under the tree, his eyes shut, waiting. The noise faded, and the clearing was still. He tried to sleep, to move to the center of the silence. Then the earth exploded and heaved him upward. Suspended in air, tumbling in slow motion, he bounced. But made no sound, his lips were sealed, his eyes squeezed shut. He'd won, death was waiting for him; death was very near at hand. That was the one certain thing that he knew. Death grabbed him by the shoulders and shook him like a rag doll, screaming in his ears, slapping his face. Rough hands closed around his arms, lifting him high. But he was not truly conscious, his eyes were closed, and it could have been a dream. He often dreamed. But the victory was his.

six

THERE WERE five of them, walking single file, moving across a wide plain. The plain had no limits, they'd left the mountain behind; a light breeze stirred the grass and made it bend. Their way was lit by stars, gloomy Orion and the dog oversaw their passage and Stringer, hands locked behind him, kept his eyes to the sky. They marched silently, ten feet apart, light-headed with exertion. The others alternated position, but Stringer always stayed in the middle. He no longer had his radio or his rifle, and he'd left his pack behind; he felt naked without his equipment, the tools of his trade. There was a pain somewhere in his body, but he did not feel it. His body was numb, when he touched his cheek there was no sensation at all. His body felt fragmented, a collection of limbs and organs held together with the thinnest glue.

They were collected inside his skin, but not coordinated in any way. His eyes ached with little explosions of light: he was unable to focus or concentrate, so he let his mind go. Floating free, a free spirit. His thoughts were tangled and confused, he was unable to separate all his ideas; he lived inside a thicket. Words and emotions came to him in fragments, of no use whatever.

They walked and then they slept, and at the end of the third day they piled into a truck. The truck materialized in the darkness and without a word the five of them climbed into it. The headlights were taped, and the truck carried no markings of any kind; it was an old vehicle, its engine barely turning over. The five of them huddled in the rear, a tangle of arms and legs; three of them immediately fell asleep and a fourth stayed awake to look after Stringer. The fourth man had a soft opaque face and blackened teeth. Stringer was given a knapsack for a pillow and urged to sleep. Urged, then ordered. The others made room for him. Someone produced a blanket though it was not cold. Stringer lay shivering on his back under the blanket and looked at various stars, fading then as dawn arrived over the plains.

He remembered the slow pace of the truck, and the silence of the men as they scanned the sky. All of the men were armed and they maintained their rifles at the ready. They were all too exhausted to speak. Pointedly ignoring him, they passed around cigarettes. He'd give anything for a cigarette, and told them that.

"Later," one of them said in the darkness. "When we've arrived."

Stringer understood the words, though he could not

identify the language. It was either English or the other language, but he thought in both of them now. There was no difference between them at all. He was unable to separate them in his head.

"Why later?" Stringer pressed. "Why not now?"

"Regulations."

"Whose?" He felt the man relax and smile. "Whose regulations?"

Stringer felt rather than understood the lie. There were plenty of cigarettes to go around, and no reason to withhold them. The other one turned away from him and nudged a companion, laughing. Well, they were bastards. At the end of the darkness, the light coming quickly now, the truck slowed and then stopped. No one moved or spoke. After a bit it started up again, traveling faster.

They talked among themselves, of inconsequential things; two of them kept sharp watch on the flanks. The mood grew brighter and almost loose, the longer they traveled. One of them finally let him have a long drag on a cigarette, then withdrew it. Sleep, they told him. Sleep now. Sleep for the rest of the journey. Stringer did not have the energy to protest.

Forty miles west of the capital the land begins to rise, first gently, then sharply, in a long escarpment. Seen from the sky the ridges roll west like waves, their crests sharp and straight as swords. In the spring and summer the slopes of the hills are deep green, and the valleys laid out in neat rectangles. No part of the land is wasted. Anonymous streams fall down the sides of the hills, cut through the shallow valleys, and eventually disappear; the water's warm, dull and thick with mud. In this district there are many small towns, some of them containing no more than a few wooden houses. The truck slipped slowly through these, its passengers taking no notice of those by the side of the road. The towns are exquisitely symmetrical, the paths straight as plumb lines, the houses severely rectangular and immaculate in the heat. They are built of dark wood, the interiors dark, the houses placed just so in shade. Gnarled trees and hopeful backyard gardens complete the impression of order and logic.

Back of the first ridge, in the vicinity of two market towns, low houses bound by wire fences sat well back of the undulating roads. A low ridge rose back of the big house. Two streams defined the land in the shape of a slice of pie. One large stream forked into two, the branches running down to the road. These might have been antecedents of the gentle Rappahannock, or any of the great war rivers; such was their pace and shape. There was a large main stream some distance to the north. The big house stood in the center of fifty hectares of land, at the end of a rutted dirt road. The house was concealed behind a stand of feathery trees. There were smaller houses and one or two large barns farther in and cattle motionless in a dark field. There were sentry posts every hundred yards, but these were not occupied.

Stringer remembered it this way. In the late afternoon he had been taken off the truck and two military men escorted him into the house. Inside, he'd collapsed and the next thing he knew he was in bed, his arms and shoulders bandaged. The room was small and brightly lit, but the windows were made very high, too high to reveal the terrain. They'd put foul-smelling unguent on his arms. Stringer prized one of the bandages loose and smelled his own burned flesh. The sight of it and the odor made him gag. There was no pain, he suspected they'd given him morphine; each morning there was blood on his pillow. He believed that they'd shaved his head. He saw himself then as a Buddha, one burned Buddha, slipped between white sheets. Unguent incense. A round, perfectly symmetrical Buddha, silent, imperturbable, sleek as marble. Stringer understood that he was light-headed and hallucinating, and fought to control it. But facts slipped away. He muttered something and looked up to see someone staring at him.

"What do you want now?"

"Nothing," Stringer said.

"Are you in pain?"

"No."

They came often, a dozen times a day. Sometimes they had other questions, complicated facts that they wanted to know. But Stringer found it difficult to put the words in order. He could not understand their meaning, he felt helpless as a child. He tried to take his memory back to the time when he was alone: the radio, the helicopters, the deep woods around him. The noise and the fire, the fury, the venom. His friend, his enemy. He tried to recall those but could not in any detailed way. The facts escaped him. When next he looked up, he was alone in the room. The door was closed.

Whatever it was, he'd gotten through it. He was damaged, but he'd survived; hurt, he was still alive. A memory that deep and disturbing was not worth recalling anyway. Let it lie, he thought. Let the lie lie. His sleep was troubled and at odd times he found himself talking aloud. Stringer was fascinated that the room appeared to be perfectly square, square dimensions, walls and windows. A paper shade hung over a bare light bulb. A carafe and a glass and an incense jar rested on a small table in the corner. His clothes were neatly piled by the door. Through a high window he saw a cloudless, blameless sky. Stringer moved his legs with difficulty, watching the white sheet rise and fall.

They knew who he was, that was for certain. They called him by name, and they spoke in the vernacular. One language or the other. They'd extracted his history, his statistics, his service record, his marriage, the places that he'd lived. Who he was, what he did. It was up-to-date and thorough. They asked him to verify the details, which he was reluctant to do; uncertain of the facts, Stringer did not want to mislead his hosts. Confused and burdened, Stringer was terrified of error. They were not insistent. They spoke of friends and of friends of friends. They were polite and competent — "sharp," Price would've said. Disciplined, determined. Stringer was unaware of the passage of time, but guessed he was not long in the hospital bed. One week, perhaps two. The attendants, helpful in every other way, could give him no clue concerning the passage of time. They were civilized but distant. They told him he'd be surprised, when he was well enough to be up and around and live with his friends. There were quite a number of them on the premises. Not an unpleasant or lurid situation, they told him. It was all quite healthy and aboveboard, and everyone cooperated.

In the evenings the residents would walk to the bridge with bamboo poles and troll for brown trout. From the bridge rail they could see the fish lying near the bottom, hanging weightless above the gravel. It was tantalizing because the fish seldom struck, although live bait was dangled in front of them. After an hour of silent fishing the residents would gather their gear and move back to the house for supper.

At the round table in the evenings Fowler sat opposite him. Monroe and Steinberg were to either side of Fowler. Two others, gray expressionless men, were to Stringer's left and right. They seldom spoke and were not otherwise identified. Unlike Fowler and Steinberg, these men were not known to Stringer. The seating never varied, although there was no written rule about it. The residents fell into line like soldiers at reveille. At first Stringer thought that Fowler wanted to keep an eye on Monroe, but there was plainly no need for that. The two others never entered in, and Monroe was preoccupied. So for conversation and amusement, Stringer played trivia games with Steinberg. He'd developed a code language, meant to deceive or mislead anyone who might be eavesdropping. He was skeptical and fearful of Fowler, who seemed to have the authority, and of the silent guards at the door. The guards were always present, even during the evening walks to the bridge. No one spoke of confinement. The games centered around the University of Chicago in the 1950s, and on jazz music. Stringer tried to trip him up.

"It's important to have the *facts,* Steinberg."

"*D'accord.*"

"For example. As an example of what I mean. You'll recall the old days, back at the 1111 Club."

"Under the El tracks on Bryn Mawr, up the street from the Edgewater Beach. Sixty-cent drinks . . ."

". . . the bandstand back of the bar. An expectant audience. When Brunis was playing at the top of his form."

"Brunies," Steinberg corrected.

"His name was legally changed to Brunis." Stringer felt Fowler's cold eyes on him.

"It was not. Among *friends,* among those who knew him best, George remained Brunies. It was a question of identity. The discographers recognized that, they understood. Dubin called him Brunies."

Dubin was a name from somewhere else. Stringer considered for a moment, then replied: "Zutty didn't."

"Zutty didn't know him in that way."

"Did. In the year 1955, Zutty held it together. The rest of them were drunk, or unawares. Zutty called him either 'George' or 'Brunis.' Depending, of course, on the occasion. Zutty had a fine sense of occasion."

"Competent authorities refer to the man as Brunies."

"Steinberg, you are full of shit."

"Your memory's too battered to remember anything, Stringer. You've gone soft. You can't get it straight. You're washed up, you're just another pebble on the beach now. It is to make me laugh. Even Fowler can see it. Fowler, give Stringer the straight scoop. Tell it to him the way it is."

Fowler dug into the hash on his plate, his eyes on the men at the door. The table was silent.

Steinberg waited, then turned back to Stringer. "All right. See if you're up to it. George Mitchell."

"Cornet."

"Alcide Pavageau?"

"Bass."

"Fitzhugh?"

"Cornet."

"Stringer, it is trumpet. Trumpet, Stringer. Trum-pet. This is a widely known fact. You've no support, Stringer."

"Sassoon."

"Come again? You're trying to slip the hook."

"Sassoon. S-a-s-s-o-o-n. What's the matter, Steinberg? Cat got your tongue? Sassoon, Steinberg! What instrument? What orchestra? When? What club? What town? Take a desperate gamble, big shot! Did he play with Ory? Was it rent-party piano on the South Side in the 1930s? Have you forgotten it already? Does your memory jog in any way? Do you hear explosions?"

Steinberg spoke quickly: "You've served up a phony name, Stringer. I never heard of any Sassoon. If the name's a phony, you spot me ten. Those are the rules, you've agreed to them."

"It's no phony, Steinberg."

"I think it's a phony and you understand the rules. As does Fowler. These rules are available to anyone who cares to read them. It's a phony, you're off your nut again. You're bats, Stringer."

"You don't remember Sassoon's refrain, do you Steinberg? It's there, but you can't find it. It's hidden, concealed behind a walking bass and clarinet riffs. Ruffles and flourishes. It's a message within a message. I'll give you a hint.

Have you forgotten yet?
Look up and swear . . .
That you'll never forget

Remember?"

"Lies, Stringer. All lies."

"Ah! But you're not sure. You have a suspicion, but you cannot make it stick. Because back in that tub of lard in the middle of your head, you remember Sassoon. Oh so vaguely. Drums. Was it drums, Steinberg? Drums maybe in the old Oliver band, the 1918 version — the one that made the rare recordings. Where the names are commonly misspelled. Where the historians depend on biased history. Where there are only one or two competent authorities, both dead. Steinberg, where are you going?"

"No support, Stringer."

"That's horseshit!"

"No."

"I've support!"

"I suppose. I suppose you do. In the same way that a hanged man supports a rope."

"That's cute, Steinberg. Adroit."

"*Au revoir.*"

"Stringer?"

He remembered Fowler's voice, low and polite, coming from across the table. Fowler put his fork on his plate, *click-click*, and leaned across the bare wood. He

166

smoothed his moustache with his forefinger and shook his head. A remonstrance. Caution. "You know the rules, Stringer. Hasn't all this gone far enough? You and Steinberg, you've been warned. Isn't there something else you can argue about? I know there are certain points of interest, meeting places, common ground. But one must be discreet. We are obliged to live by the rules that we have. These rules are for our own protection. The repetition of the names of musicians . . . might be . . ."

"Yes."

"Misconstrued. I've mentioned it before."

"I suppose it is a bit boring for all of you here."

Fowler sighed. "More than a bit, Mr. Stringer."

"I'll speak to Steinberg about it."

"We don't want you to *repress*, Mr. Stringer. But surely . . ."

"It'll be a different game at breakfast, we're anxious to please. We'll put together a whole new category of conversation. Assemble an entirely new classification. Believe you me. Something novel, something chewy. You'll be able to get your teeth into it."

"I'd appreciate that, so would they. All of us would."

Monroe nodded, smiling. He was a thin light-haired man with a useless right arm. His right arm stayed in his lap, the fingers bent into a claw. He grinned at Fowler.

"Roger that," Stringer said.

"And don't disturb Steinberg further tonight."

"No, no."

"You know what I mean."

"It was nothing to do with me. Sassoon did it. Steinberg finished Sassoon off with Lenin."

"Of course."

"He couldn't remember. It itched him, pissed him off. He's up in his room now, going through the documents. He'll find what he's looking for, but he'll have some bad moments. He's searched before, the search is familiar to him. Familiar but troublesome. Steinberg's no stranger to investigations."

Fowler left the room then, and the rest of them fell silent. When he returned he was cheerful. "Well, well. Good, good." He rubbed his hands together. "So let's adjourn. Everybody, take your tea and let's move on to the common room. We'll pick up right where we left off. No missing pages. How does that sound? Everybody satisfied? Mr. Stringer, why don't you sit over there, in the chair near the fire. There'll be just the five of us, is that all right? Now tonight there's nothing planned, we're all free form. Interrupt when you feel like it, but only when the speaker has finished his thought and paused. He *must pause*. Two beats. Uh-one-anda-two. Remember? And we must all speak distinctly. I believe that Mr. Monroe has the floor. I believe we were listening to his account when we broke up last night." Fowler turned to the two men sitting by the table at the door and watched as they took out notebooks and pencils and arranged them neatly. Expressionless, they waited. Then Fowler turned back to the residents. "Does everyone have what they need? Cigarettes? Tea? Poke the fire, Mr. Stringer. It's chilly in this room. Lead off, Major Monroe. You have the floor. We're all listening. All ears. Continue. Begin where you left off."

Then Fowler switched on the tape recorder and for a

168

moment all Stringer could hear was the whir of gears and the squeak of the tape. When Monroe began to speak, Steinberg reappeared and settled himself on the bench near the window.

He remembered the climbing, the long walks in the hot sun. The sun dazzling, the heat heavy and damp. He was never alone. There were hills in the distance but he could not see them because of the closeness of the vegetation. At night he inspected leaves' veins, phosphorescent with decay. His body drained, his feet were hard to lift; he listened for night noises. He attempted to stay alert, but his eyes were forced downward, to touch the ground. He was always thirsty, always hot in the head, and his skin was slimy to the touch. He stank. Crossing streams he moved at an angle to the current; when he reached midstream he was cautious and kept his eyes up and watchful, waiting for movement. In the water his shoulders hurt, the sweat dribbled down his back in rivulets. Insects attacked his face, the repellent was worse than useless. He stoically moved ahead. Shrubs and small trees overlapped the water, so the streams were undefined. There were no limits of width and length, and their surfaces were mirrored. He was always quiet and careful while walking or climbing. He heard only the rustle of his own clothing, and the heave of his breath.

"Why did you keep on?"

"Persistence."

"So it must have been pleasant in its way."

"Was, I guess."

"You were not put upon?"

"No."

"Do you have any association with it now? What does it bring to mind, if it brings anything to mind. You can speak plainly."

"The green of the spring," Stringer said, and smiled.

"You can't forget it?"

"Or remember it."

"Well . . ."

"Either one."

"Let's go back to the helicopters. There had to've been a guidance . . ."

"These were assignments."

". . . some prearranged . . ."

"Naturally."

"I'm fascinated by helicopters. That wasn't my line, you know. How did they decide *where* to put you down? What was the procedure behind that? Who made the decision?"

"Command."

"Alone?"

"So far as I know."

"That seems odd. Doesn't it seem odd to you?"

Stringer smiled.

"Not odd?" Fowler asked.

"Well, I assume there were other . . . inputs."

"What would those be? And on what evidence? What kind of intelligence was there? Human or electronic? You see, it would be very helpful to us if you could discuss the mechanism. The *process*. I mean step by step. Details, facts. That would be very helpful indeed."

In the morning, each morning, Stringer'd present himself at Fowler's office. Fowler sat behind a small desk. There were two mirrors in the room, each reflecting the other, and the desk was covered with papers. Fowler usually said very little; he often glanced at the mirror to his right, then consulted the papers on his desk. He reminded Stringer of a military bureaucrat, secure in paperwork and obedient to his superiors. Once he lectured Stringer on his responsibilities, Stringer's responsibilities to himself and to his comrades. Everyone was interdependent and had responsibilities of some kind. He, Fowler, had a job to do like everyone else. Everyone had his job. Fowler's was to ask questions, Stringer's to answer them.

The room, though small and airless, was not intimidating in any way. Fowler, nondescript in a gray tunic, sat with the papers in front of him and occasionally made a note in shorthand or in code. His fingers were heavy and stained with nicotine, and occasionally they trembled; he seemed physically vulnerable, though his voice was confident and his face hard-set. Fowler was friendly, and spoke in an accented vernacular. At their first meeting he'd explained that he was originally a mountain man, from the western part of the country, near Oregon. He was the great-grandson of pioneers. But he had not been back in many years and doubted now that he would ever go back. He'd made his choice and was satisfied. He was no longer a criminal or associated with criminals, his conscience was clear. He told Stringer that his reputation had preceded him, there was no reason why they could not get along. Was he remembered in any way?

Did Command have an official explanation for his abrupt disappearance? Stringer tried to recall what Command had said, and Steinberg's theory. Fowler waited patiently for an answer, and when none came he shook his head and smiled; no matter.

Fowler smiled his cracked smile and said it was easy to talk once a man got used to it. He was an expert at drawing men out, encouraging them to speak freely and accurately. It was important that Stringer understand his own motives and the motives of his comrades. Fowler was his friend, he wanted to help. But they needed facts, and those facts had to be placed in context. In other words, they needed to know everything about the process. He and Stringer, they were compatriots. They shared a heritage.

"Do you have a family here?" Stringer asked.

"I live alone," Fowler said.

"But you're free to come and go."

"Entirely free. I suppose they told you I was a prisoner of some kind."

"No, it was a mystery."

"Command said that?"

"Command said nothing, it was all double-talk with Command. Steinberg had one or two theories, as I recall."

"Poor Steinberg." Fowler shook his head in disapproval. "He's in trouble. No, I'll tell you the truth. This was entirely a question of free choice, how I came to be here. My own choice, freely made. I'm committed absolutely. I'm not saying that the choice was easy or safe, no; but there was no forcing. I've undertaken a number of important studies, with the help of men like you. They've called me a traitor, and believe I'll return. But I won't. I'm here, and I intend to stay."

Stringer nodded politely and accepted the cigarette Fowler offered. They were silent for a moment. Then, "Don't you miss anything?"

"It's no secret that in the beginning I missed the West, where my roots are. My people settled there in the middle of the last century, arriving over the mountains in covered wagons. In my part of the country, we're a very old family. Still own good mountain land, and farm it." Fowler paused, watching Stringer. "But that was in another time. The frontier now is right here, not there."

"I appreciate the cigarette."

"We'll get down to cases now."

Stringer was distracted and shaken, thinking of the West. The burly mountains, the limitless green of the valleys; the wilderness, untouched and unspoiled, kingdoms to settle. To cross the Sierra Nevada in the dead of winter was an act of pure heroic faith. Stringer shook his head, trying to free it of the image Fowler'd introduced. It frightened him, that time bore no relation to this. There was no link. They were two quite separate and distinct worlds, unbridged and unbridgeable by men. Fowler leaned across the desk, the buttons of his open tunic touching the papers. He grinned, waiting for Stringer to answer. But Stringer was silent, imprisoned in his memory.

"We'll get down to cases now. In due course, I'll file a report to my superiors. The authorities here. It will be as complete and objective as I can make it, everything that

173

can be known will be known. Your dossier. Dated. Numbered. You'll cease to be private, Stringer."

Stringer shook his head, no.

"Oh, yes. You'll like it. Nothing concealed or withheld. You'll be surprised at the number of files we have, and the help they've been. You've important information that will aid us. You, Stringer. You alone." Fowler smiled, and ended softly. "You're worth a battalion of troops."

The sessions were brief. After no more and often less than an hour, the conversation concluded, Stringer would excuse himself and leave. Others were waiting. He had no remaining obligations and would quit the building for an hour's walk in the woods. Fowler stood at attention in the doorway, watching him go.

Outside, Stringer walked slowly down the dirt road. Game was so plentiful, it was a tragedy he had no gun. For a while he carried a long stick and practiced flushing birds. It was difficult to do without a dog, but Stringer's eyes were excellent and he could spot movement twenty yards ahead. His eyes darted from the trees to the ground and he knew the habits of game birds. The birds were large and sometimes sluggish. But he felt witless, lifting the stick to his shoulder and firing.

Bang.

Bang bang.

There was always someone nearby.

There was one place back of the big house, a hollow near the bend of the river on the edge of the property. The hollow was cool and dark, huge trees protected it from the sun. On most occasions Steinberg was there before him, sitting quietly beside the water. He'd stand on the rim of the hollow, like a sentry, hidden by the trees, and watch silent Steinberg. Then he would leave, a man was entitled to his privacy. Poor Steinberg did not like company in the mornings, he was up early and talking to Fowler; his appointment was Fowler's first. Later, Steinberg drifted away to walk in the woods and fetch up finally on the banks of the stream. At these times Stringer would walk away west to the bridge and look at the fish and talk to whomever was about. The two others were often there, along with the guards; they went to the bridge in the mornings to tie flies. The flies were never used, but placed in a large white box; one would hold the hook while the other tied the fly. They worked very slowly, helping each other; there were two kinds of flies, red and black. These two, so gray, so anonymous, were monosyllabic talkers, a condition Stringer found difficult. In an effort to coax something from them (were they friends or enemies?) he spoke candidly of his life — revealing forgotten personal details, posing difficult questions. He told them a good deal about his wife, how they had met and courted and married and ultimately parted. He attempted to describe her to them, but found he'd forgotten what she looked like; nor could he recall how she'd been in bed. Good, bad, indifferent — what? He wondered if she thought about how he'd "been" . . . in bed. Odd, but the thought provoked no desire in him.

The twins — he thought of these two as twins, doubles, so alike — always hastened away, and Stringer was left alone. After an hour, he'd return to the hollow knowing that in the meantime Steinberg had vanished. He made

his way down the slope to the stream and sat on a dry
log at the edge of the water and watched the current, the
eddies and bits and pieces that floated by. Often a fish
broke water. He stared at the current until he could no
longer stand it, then went back to the house for lunch.

"Later," Stringer would promise as he walked away.

His position was this. Stringer kept everything open.
That was the point of it. He kept all his charts available,
and any course could be corrected; he'd made that quite
plain to Fowler. It was the way he intended to live, missing nothing of value. He did not think of himself as bound
or tied in any way; he was free. Only the end was pre-
determined but Stringer pushed that out of his mind,
having exhausted its possibilities. It had nothing to do
with the situation. He thought that even if forced he
could maneuver inside the obligation. There was room
enough, even in the largest organizations. Fowler knew
that, too. He did not care to close off his routes. He
thought there could always be a new career or a new
marriage or a new place to live in, and nothing could
decisively alter his life or the chances that he took; life
was self-renewing, although this was not anything that
he cared to dwell on. Danger was part of it, he had never
known a time when fear and danger were not present in
their various forms. He guarded himself against shock of
any kind, being careful with Fowler and the others who
questioned him. If he kept his nerve, the pieces would
drop into place. The point was not to hold back but to get
up close, as one dealt with an unpredictable animal. If
they sensed you were frightened, they would begin to
stalk you. They'd run your legs off and you'd never see

them. You'd run to the ends of the earth and still not be safe or know peace. Up close was the safest haven, but it had its dangers; and he was facing those now. The danger was in shock and discovery: risks increased the closer you got, and this was true for airplane pilots or writers or soldiers or lovers, all of which he had been or contemplated being at one time or another. He was trained, he knew his job. At a certain point nerve and sheer competence would win out over misfortune, or fate. He'd kept all his routes open, but Stringer could not recall what he had been the last time. Exactly what he had been and where, and what Fowler was after. Fowler was exploring his mind, he was on an expedition into the interior. So Stringer considered it necessary to remain at the edge of the precipice. That was what he thought about sitting on the log, watching the stream. The tributary of the big river, opaque, soft, mysterious, old. Watching time and space move out from under him, he was afraid; with nothing closed off there were too many chances to be taken, too many possibilities.

In the evenings after supper, Stringer and Steinberg were sometimes able to move off alone. This was after the questioning, when the tape was exhausted. Steinberg was good about letting the conversation wander, though wary of Fowler and the others. It was necessary to keep Stringer off-balance. Stringer thought that the talk was a means of connection to another world, his and Steinberg's ancient history.

"Steinberg, do you remember the Compass?"

"Partly."

"Bud on draught, Meister Brau in bottles. The stage at the rear of the bar, leatherette banquettes. Noisy urinals. The bartender's name was Gus."

"No, not Gus. Gus was the bartender of the place on Rush."

"Right, Steinberg. Your memory's returned. The bartender's name was Larry. A graduate student in linguistics, he wrote the orders in root languages. Surely you remember Larry."

"No, I'm sorry to correct you a second time. Larry tended bar at another place, and that place was on Rush as well. This bar was somewhat fancier than the others, if you'll recall. A different clientele: all those narrow-brim hats and fat wallets from Michigan Avenue. You'll remember it if you think about it. That was a bar for advertising men. At the Compass, the bartender's name was Bob."

"Just so. Do you remember Nichols and May, Steinberg?"

"Of course."

"You were in the law school then, it was difficult for you to leave your books for an evening. There were other things, significant obligations. There was competition for your time, Steinberg."

"But nevertheless . . . I remember Nichols and May."

". . . I thought of it as an incident, an episode. You never told them to go fuck themselves, as you should've done. Of course both of them were cool as ice chips, and talented. And the others with them, the Compass players."

"Well said, Stringer."

". . . now this is the crux. I think if we are to begin at the beginning, we must begin at the Compass. *Comprenez?* This was something entirely new, and it was happening in our time, in our town, at our university. A comedian taking chances with the public, taking his themes *from the audience*. It was new and novel. Now, there was something of the politician in Nichols and May, wouldn't you agree to that, Steinberg? Incredible, really. Daring, what they did."

"Yes, it was so new and novel and daring that they were doing it in the sixteenth century. In Shakespeare's time, Stringer, they made up dramas from suggestions of the audience. An audience of kings and their courts. It is to laugh. You've got the times out of joint again. It would be a grave mistake for you to consider the Compass the beginning of anything."

"And funny! Hilarious! It was pleasant in its way to sit at the bar with a Bud and laugh at Nichols and May, who improvised." Stringer was silent for a moment, lost in thought; Steinberg waited. "In those years the University of Chicago had every turn of mind, all the new angles. Stalinoids! Trotskyites! Pot! Lonely crowds! Willing women! Deft and crafty comedians! And free love, Steinberg. Free. Love."

"We didn't get any."

"No bill was ever presented. Free love for the asking!"

Steinberg was silent, watching Stringer with hooded eyes.

"Nichols and May in the forefront, the leading edge, at the Compass. They played to the crowd, brought it to its feet, tears of laughter. *Some of their laughs were in bad taste.* They angered the powers that be. These were brave transactions."

"Stringerstringerstringer. You don't know what you're saying. You don't understand anything."

"Well, we were in at the start of something new. We should've stayed, Steinberg. If we'd've stayed, everything would have been hunky-dory. We'd've been on top of things, rooted. Rooted in our time, a beautiful improvisation. Boone understood it, there's no question in my mind of that. He saw the light. Steinberg, just one question by the way. Why did we leave the university when we did? In that particular direction. And then later . . ."

"Don't push it, Stringer. Please."

"An innocent enough question. It's innocent, Steinberg!"

"Stringer?"

" 'Bye-bye, Steinberg."

Then Fowler was at his elbow, looming over him. The other two were at the door. He watched Steinberg retreat slowly, his head wagging. He thought Steinberg looked beaten. Fowler spoke in a low voice: "Now I've asked you before, Mr. Stringer. They are going to lean on us, so you shut up. Jazz and Chicago are *out of bounds.* They are out of bounds for reasons you know as well as I. Steinberg isn't responsible, you know the regulations. I'm the responsible authority here. Keep your conversation general or you'll pay the consequences. No more games . . ."

"Steinberg?"

"He's out of range."

"I can see him near the coatrack. Do come back, Steinberg! (Fowler, you should have seen him in the prime of his time.)"

"Yes . . ."

"Fowler, you don't understand. It was a simple stab at history, Steinberg and I knew it all. This was just a move to jog Steinberg's memory. He knows it better than I, I was only in residence one year. Steinberg was a fixture, he spent seven years on the South Side of Chicago. A very fancy wonderful place it was then, quite unlike the schools to the east and west. We were moving on. I've seen nothing its equal since. And now, at the end of the line, Steinberg's turned into a recluse. There he is, near the hat rack. A concerned gentleman, a former scholar, the university life-force."

". . . but just like you now."

"No, not that."

"Yes, exactly like that."

"You've got it wrong."

Fowler bent his head over Stringer's chair, solicitous. "Well, well. Good, good," he said. "I believe Mr. Steinberg has retired for the evening." He surveyed the silent group of men. "We should all be in bed shortly. Everybody, let's move on to the common room. We'll pick up right where we left off. How does that hit you? Everybody satisfied? Let's move three chairs into a circle. You take the chair in the middle, Mr. Monroe . . ."

"Steinberg!"

"No shouting, Mr. Stringer."

"STEINBERG!" Stringer looked around him and saw that the others were gone. Fowler had summoned the two by the door, and now they stood over him, solemn, thick-waisted. He instinctively covered his head with his arms, and then he heard Fowler's dry laugh.

"Now you come and sit quietly for a moment. Just for a moment. It's coming out all right. Mr. Steinberg will be here presently to give an accounting. And in the meantime you can talk with me. I'll turn on the machine, so we'll have company. So we won't forget anything. Yes, like that. Quiet now. The others have gone, they're in the common room now. We can sit here and talk among ourselves, no pressure or confusion or fear of being overheard. Yes, the candles give a nice soft light. Almost time to retire, don't you think? The hour's late, it's quiet and serene, in no way cause for alarm. No need for worry. Now you think for a minute. You put your mind in a comfortable place. We're going to do something new. You're going to tell me all about it. Say the first things that come into your head, try not to cogitate too much. The very first things. Steinberg's upstairs now, no cause for worry or alarm."

. . . .

"I didn't hear."

. . . .

"You can say anything you want, but I didn't hear that. Don't think about these others here. They've nothing to do with us. You know my hearing, you're going to have to speak up a little. Not loud, just up a little. Now, what comes into your mind when I mention Command?"

"Bomb."

"Command again."

"Soldier."

"Command."

182

. . . .

"I couldn't hear, Mr. Stringer. You speak up."

. . . .

"Well, fine, Mr. Stringer. Let me give you a cup of tea now. And a cigarette. You drink this, you'll feel fine. Let me light the cigarette for you. Tell me one thing, man to man. Steinberg's your friend. A friend and a comrade-in-arms. Now tell me this, was he a good soldier?"

"The best."

"What exactly did he do?"

"We never knew each other's missions."

"But you knew him well."

"I didn't know him well, no one *knows* Steinberg. Except we were acquainted more than slightly at the University of Chicago. We had a mutual friend named Boone who had a fine case of the bats. Not uncommon in those days. He was two years ahead, I'd see him on the Midway. Steinberg was a big man on the campus of the University of Chicago. Into everything. I got married and Steinberg went away to Washington. I didn't see him for quite some little time after that. But I knew him back when, everyone did."

"But then he became a soldier."

"Well, of course. Any idiot knows that."

"How, then?" Fowler leaned into him.

Backing away, Stringer said: "It was one of the things that happened, in lighthearted moments. One of the objectives. One of the things that you did if you felt like it and weren't derailed. If you got the breaks."

"What exactly did Steinberg —"

"His reputation preceded him."

183

"How did it do that, Mr. Stringer? How did it precede him? Details, please."

"Write-ups in the paper. Steinberg was a hero, you heard his name wherever you went. Living legend. He was displayed to tourists, at one point in his career. Then Steinberg went underground and you didn't hear anything any more. There are ways and means to do this if you know how, and Steinberg knew how. He was as far underground as a man can get."

"Yes, his name was known to me. I may have met him at one time or another."

"You can take my word for it."

"But there are puzzles. I'd heard of him, I knew the name. I know the chain of command pretty well. But you should see my files, Mr. Stringer. I've all these files, and Steinberg doesn't appear in them anywhere. Isn't that odd? All this paper, and no Steinberg."

"He wouldn't've been *recorded* in any way. No. Highest Levels forbade it. You can take my word for that."

"Yes."

"My word's good."

"Of course."

"Generals knew him by name."

"But I'd like to know about the organization. That's what we're here for, Mr. Stringer. That's what these other gentlemen are interested in. The organization and how it worked. You can supply that information and satisfy everyone. You can tell what you know about the organization, what was recorded and what was not, and how you and Steinberg fitted into it."

"That's hard."

184

"It shouldn't be."

"I've explained it. Different outfits. I was in one, he was in another. I mean it was the same outfit, but different units. We knew each other's work by the grapevine, it exists in the army. I'm sure you've heard of it. Back-channel stuff."

"Odd, I had the impression that Steinberg was a civilian. Attached . . . you know what I mean? I understood he was on the civil side."

"That's a goddamned lie!"

"Well, I know that now. After talking to you. Still, it's odd, isn't it?"

"Get it straight, then."

"Tell me the details, the mechanics. Tell me how it worked. Imagine that you are describing a machine's various parts. Tell me about some of Mr. Steinberg's exploits?"

Stringer paused to light a cigarette. He wanted to protect Steinberg to the extent that it was possible to do so. It was difficult for him to separate what was sensitive and private from what was not, to conceal and withhold the proper information. Fowler's questions confused him.

". . . exploits?"

"In the first place, it's *Colonel* Steinberg," Stringer ventured, buying time. "Perhaps was light colonel, my memory's faded. There was a time, Steinberg was in the command chopper and some men were in the deepshit. Steinberg landed the bird in the middle of the men and took them out. He did that under concentrated fire in circumstances that were shocking. It wasn't always easy to distinguish between friends and enemies. All of it was done under fire, quick as a wink. It was conceivable that he was shot down once by one of his own men. A tragedy if true, but possible. This was one of the legends that surrounded Steinberg. It's awkward to speak of it further, as a military man you'll understand and appreciate the restrictions. I believe it was some time later. That they took the unit away from him. That must have been it. It was after this particular incident . . ."

"Relieved of command?" Fowler asked sharply.

"No! That didn't happen. That was something else altogether. Not Steinberg. Nothing was ever taken away from Steinberg."

"Well, you've filled in one of the blanks. It's possible he'd come down . . . for you?"

"He caught a slug somewhere."

"From your rifle, Stringer."

"No . . ."

"I think that was the way it was. A natural mistake. No reason to brood over this incident in any way. The circumstances were confusing. It was a mistake that could happen to anybody. Did you work together often?"

"Where did you get that idea?"

"Something that you said. You know the details, Stringer. You've a command of the facts. You know the code . . . and the other things."

"Well, it was a big war. Bigger than people thought."

"Yes. About working together."

"That's the army for you."

"The code —"

"It shook us up when we learned what happened to him."

"Who?"

"Steinberg."

"I've forgotten just now. It's slipped my mind. What was it that happened?"

"Christ, don't you people ever read the newspapers? Don't you give one good damn what happens? There were displays everywhere. Special ceremonies . . . news reports. Jesus, to forget something like that! It's criminal!"

"Yes, I'm sorry," Fowler said patiently. "But it seems to have slipped my mind."

. . . .

"Yes?"

"You people, you're careless."

"Yes."

"It doesn't have any meaning for you."

"The details, please."

Stringer wet his lips and lit another cigarette. He tried to remember the details they'd worked out. Or that he'd worked out, Steinberg remaining silent and uncommunicative, believing that the cause was hopeless. And that Fowler was a dangerous enemy. Stringer nodded, he'd risk everything now. He saw Steinberg watching them from a corner of the room. "Well, he was lost and never found. Lost in action, he was an MIA. I guess for a week there wasn't an airplane in the theater that wasn't out looking for Steinberg. He was so valuable, you see. And popular! Everybody was out beating the bush. Command'd assembled a task force. The son of a gun just disappeared. Some action he was in, he'd gotten in over his head. No details were ever released, and that ought to give you an idea of the importance of it. The security. The details are locked in the computers and the filing cabinets . . ."

"And where are they?"

Stringer gave him a name.

"Spell that."

Stringer spelled it out.

"Go on now."

". . . and very highly classified. Steinberg flew in with the chopper and that was the last anybody heard. Good soldier, I remember him as he was. Imagine my surprise . . ."

"And never found."

". . . when he turned up here. Big as life."

"Well, you shot him down."

"No —"

"Yes, that was the way it was. You arrived here by different routes. You shot him down, that was exactly the way it was."

"No, never found. Still listed as MIA, that's according to regulations. Poor Steinberg. The army lost some hell of a fighting man. They'd give dearly to know where he is now. He might've gone all the way, that's what they said. He got *everything* — Legion of Merit, Silver Star, the works. They were not stingy, and the citations were heartwarming. Great American. Great patriot. Brave. Resourceful."

"Come off it, Stringer!"

"It's the truth!"

"Facts!"

"It's God's truth."

"You fucking well get down to details." Fowler's voice came at him sharp as knives.

"For Christ's sake, if it weren't true would I be sitting here telling you all this? Giving you the facts. Shit, get it straight!"

"You know where you are, Stringer."

"I know it."

"We don't have to do that drill, do we."

"No, no."

"You shot the son of a bitch *down*, Stringer. Sharpshooting. You can see the results there, look to the other side of the room. The man on the bench, your buddy Steinberg. Those are the results of your little crack-up. Of course it is possible that Steinberg is in better shape than you are." Fowler grinned. "That's possible, indeed likely —"

"No, no," Stringer's voice was barely audible.

"We go where the facts lead us. There's no escaping facts."

"It didn't happen, I had no idea."

"No excuses, Stringer."

"Excuses?" He was helpless now.

"We've evidence." Fowler looked at Steinberg, whose face was turned to the wall.

Stringer shook his head, No. He wouldn't believe it. He'd give them everything else, but he wouldn't give them that. He and Steinberg, they'd endured together for a generation. They'd gone the distance. Steinberg sat slumped on the bench, motionless. Stringer tried to reach him.

". . . so you get straight on the details. You imagine it

the way it was, no false leads. Names and numbers. Places. Dates. Codes. Missions. A simple five-figure code, wasn't it?"

"Five or six, depending on the days of the month."

"Which for which?"

"Six on odds, five on evens," Stringer lied. He saw Steinberg look away. He thought that Steinberg was smiling, but could not be sure.

"Well, you think about that again," Fowler said. "You let your mind go over the details."

"Well, it's impossible to do that."

"What was the mission?"

"We never knew."

"Stringer, you bastard."

"It's God's truth."

"Where did Steinberg come from?"

"Wasted effort."

"The *place*."

"How can I do this? How can I imagine what happened to Steinberg, there's no percentage there at all. Steinberg's his own man, always has been. I'm another article altogether. There would be no way for me to do a thing of that kind."

"You see those two over there?" Fowler pointed at the door.

"I don't want to hear about it."

"Those two. The way they go about it. It's interesting, Stringer. Look at them. Look at their hands."

"I'm not listening."

"Sometime . . . the war . . ." Fowler's voice faded.

"He was a missing person."

"I'd like to know your opinion." Fowler was far away now.

"You don't know anything about the war. Your type knows nothing. Not a damned thing."

Into focus again: "Exactly, I want to help. We all do, and you can give us a hand. You can help me clarify my own views. You tell me the details. You tell me, then I'll know."

"Not from me."

"Yes, I think so. I think you will."

"Not secondhand." Stringer fought for his equilibrium, the room was dark, Fowler behind him now. Stringer thought he was protected, he'd built a wall between his mind and his memory. It was important to him that nothing escape, that he give nothing away. He watched Steinberg on the bench at the end of the room, and the two others walking slowly toward him. He put his arms over his head. "You can forget about it," Stringer said.

The days passed smoothly, without serious incident. The atmosphere now was peaceful, in the autumn a mist developed around the stream in the hollow. The air was soft enough to touch. Some days, when Steinberg reached the place first, Stringer would lie back among the trees and watch him. Steinberg had taken to whittling sticks. His knife was hidden at the base of one of the feathery trees. Steinberg whittled sticks into sharp-pointed styluses, then went about writing in the soft earth near the stream. Often he'd write for an hour or more, writing a sentence then scratching it out, smoothing the earth and beginning again. When he finished writing he broke the point of the stylus and tossed it in the stream, where it would drift downcurrent. Then he carefully replaced the knife at the base of the tree, and walked off.

This was familiar to Stringer. He enjoyed staying back among the trees, out of sight. He could see Steinberg, but Steinberg couldn't see him. He never looked around. When he was writing with the stylus he wrote with complete self-possession, kneeling on the ground and bending, like a traveler inspecting a map. Stringer thought that he looked like an old man at prayer, an old Oriental, leaning toward the east, or whatever it was that they did to give them strength. Leaning toward the sun, old bones showing in outline through a coarse cotton shirt. The sentences were scrupulously etched — then erased. When Steinberg got up to go, Stringer would reveal himself, Steinberg's sentinel. His watchman, his lookout. But the other man never glanced around; he threw his stick in the water and stalked off, lonely, preoccupied.

Vanishing Steinberg.

He refused to understand the dilemma, though Stringer attempted to explain it to him. It was quite simple, really. He was trapped. The memory was too valuable to let go and too painful to keep. In that way, Stringer said, it was like an inherited fortune to a man who feared and hated money.

"You can pretend it isn't there, Stringer," Steinberg said.

"That is not helpful."

"It's true. You'd best learn."

"Easily said, Steinberg."

"That's what you'd best do. Do that, don't listen to Fowler."

Stringer wanted to ask a question, but didn't. In any case, Steinberg refused to discuss the matter further. He preferred the closed world of the hollow and the stream, both of mysterious origins and endings. Witnesses to martial history, Steinberg said. They were not permitted off the property, they did not know the source of the water or its destination. Fowler'd point vaguely to the hills, when asked — *there*, he'd say. *In that vicinity.* And grinning, he'd turn away. After a time, Stringer and Steinberg ceased to worry about it, though they often wondered where they were. Fowler's mysteries were an annoyance. But the hollow was a comfortable and convenient place to be, regulations aside, when reviewing personal history. That was what Stringer did, sitting on the banks of the stream. His own life drifted by in fragments, bits and pieces of memory, hard to hold. Chicago and the university were clear enough, clear as panes of window glass: Hyde Park–Kenwood, the Midway, the Compass Bar on a Tuesday night, the laughter and the uproar (it was an island in the center of an island). He was unable to get straight what happened after Chicago, although it had to do with the government and the war. He did not probe too deeply, mindful of hazard. He thought he remembered buying a trench coat at Brooks Brothers, he and Steinberg laughing about the color and the fit, the depth of the center vent, the epaulets.

Steinberg later immortalized the purchase of the trench coat:

Hey, Mike! Guy goes to Brooks to buy a trench coat, girl waits on him. Modest laughter, Nichols and May considering the problem, withdrawing to a corner of the stage, talking together for a minute.

Mike, there's more! There's a social history, metaphors, scenarios, conundrums. Main currents of American thought, Mike, this man is a spy! They've drafted him, signed him up. He's done his training, now he's buying his uniform. It's the second floor of the store on Madison Street, across from the Chicago Athletic Club. You get the picture? A gray day in the Loop. Clubmen all around, brokers in banker's gray. Understand? He's regarded with respect and affection, this spy. He has a secret that no-body knows. There's a war on! The Compass is warm and smoky, everybody's laughing. The place is like a house party, or a private bar; the customers first-name the bartender. Mike and Elaine onstage trying to make it out, trying to fit the pieces together. Steinberg's satisfied, sitting at the bar with a wise and contemptuous smile, sipping Bud.

They've told him everything about the war, except where it is and what it does! What it's for! Who's in it! When it starts! And what it looks like! But he's eager to please, Mike. And he wants the girl to see that, he wants the girl to see how eager he is. How well he'll meet the challenge. It's a war and he's determined to belong to it. It's his! Everyone is laughing now, getting set. Mike and Elaine onstage, wary, watching the audience. A prop. Who has a trench coat for a prop? A brown raincoat comes sailing up onto the stage from a table in the rear, amid laughter and applause. Spotlights up, the bar falls

194

silent. Steinberg is silent and scowling, waiting for them. He'd given them everything that they need, he's a brilliant one, that Steinberg. Graduate student of law, amateur logician. Suddenly Nichols moves stage left and begins to speak in his cracked-glass voice, and the laughter begins again. Elaine's wringing her hands and chewing her lower lip, eyes darting and fearful. She's afraid of a man who needs a trench coat. Whatever for? It's funny, and tears spring to the eyes of the audience. The laughter rises around Steinberg, and he permits himself a smile. The memory of this is as clear as it's possible for memory to be.

He tried to separate the parts, to follow Fowler's advice. To understand the future, Fowler'd warned, he had to understand the past. Not the theory, the details. He had not avoided the war, that much was certain. But he did not seek it out, either. That was his first mistake, he'd permitted the war to come to him. His war duty was determined by a machine and by Steinberg; those were facts. There was no choice involved. It was a question of numbers, and a man with a vision. They posted him in strange places. He lived on a post in the plains in the middle of one summer, the horizon out of reach. They gave him special quarters, and permission to use the O Club. No rank, *Mr.* Stringer this, *Mr.* Stringer that. There were occasional messages from the elusive Steinberg, who normally traveled under cover of some sort. Then he lived abroad and took long holidays, skiing in Australia once. He was happy enough, according to the memory that he had. The memory was pleasant, what there was of it.

They cut his orders at the beginning of one month, and he was gone at the end of the next. This was after the year in language school, in California. He lived in various places the first year, he could not recall their names. Steinberg was elsewhere, highly regarded in his line of work. They were *all* highly regarded, the unit so small and elite they disregarded rank; morale was high. Why not? They were university men, experts. They rotated assignments every six months. He was a headquarters man the first tour, then he was detailed to SAG. More training (on an island then, a misnamed rockpile off the coast of Maine), a rotation to Washington, finally returned to the war. SAG was engaged in difficult missions. It was an honor, a feather in his cap, or so he was told. The unit was picked by hand, and strictly volunteer. Wasn't that it? He remembered that the company was independent, operating under control of Command. They looked on him as a veteran, someone dependable. He spoke the language, he knew the terrain. His unit operated in the mountains, in the most remote part of the country. They'd go weeks without seeing the enemy, and when they saw him, they'd withdraw. Plant the black boxes and retreat; radio Command and withdraw as quickly as they were able, back to the place where the helicopters could get them. Sometimes they had to fight their way back, but not often. An intimate unit, only eighty men; a band of brothers, playing a game of cat and mouse. The mission was elusive.

Command's name was lost to him, if he ever knew it. He could not recollect the names of his friends, nor the towns where they operated. These facts were gone, though others remained. The terrain stuck with him, the hills in the distance and the closeness of the air; the canopy of trees, shutting out the light. The insects, the heat; the long descents down mountainsides, the weight on his back. The numbers he was obliged to keep in his head, on instant call. There was that, and the one brilliant afternoon, and the nightmare followed by a day of white light, a fire in his brain. The earth spun, dreamy in slow motion; his nostrils stung, and his fingers were numb. Later he feared the night, he who had feared nothing; who had cared for nothing and examined nothing, and therefore feared nothing. He knew in advance the nights when he'd dream and fought to stay awake. To remain invulnerable, behind barriers. He concentrated on the future and talked to the ceiling; he fought to laugh, summoning the lurid, the grotesque, and the sentimental. Sweet nights in the mountains of New Hampshire or riotous ones on the Midway. But always, sometime before dawn, he'd succumb, embrace the night, and wait for a vision of hecatombs.

After two years, Stringer troubled Fowler for explanations. You'll have to report *progress*, Fowler, or admit some measure of weakness and inadequacy. That must be quite a dossier by now, how many pages would it be? And how dog-eared? And the contradictions, so many of those. So many facts, impressions, definitions, anecdotes, recollections. The personal effects of Stringer. In reply, Fowler was soothing but distant. He'd exhausted his questions, his assignment was over, and Stringer had no satisfaction. No escape was possible, so Stringer was obliged to relent though he did not yield. For a time he wrote letters of protest, then abandoned those as well. He stayed on in the house near the capital, in the mountains. The seasons changed. The twins disappeared and Monroe died. Two others replaced the twins, and of course Steinberg remained.

In the evenings when it was warm, Stringer and Steinberg went to the bridge alone to fish for brown trout. They'd fish for an hour, and Steinberg would leave. The others never left the house, and they had the grounds to themselves. They continued to go at each other with trivia from the University of Chicago in the 1950s, and from the world of jazz music. Fowler no longer cared what they did; he put the tape recorder away and took his meals elsewhere. The guards remained, less visible than before. The pattern was familiar now, Stringer would reach Steinberg with an obscure musician, someone he'd never heard of or someone fictitious. Or he'd remember quotable comedy at the Compass on a Tuesday night. Steinberg was stronger now and strangely cheerful, and in the early evenings he gave as good as he got. But in the end the responsibility was too great, and he would fall silent and try to change the conversation; finally he'd quit the table, to rummage among the documents in his room. Next morning, though, the two would be fit, right as rain, all disputes forgotten. And walk arm in arm to the hollow, where Stringer stood silent guard while Steinberg scratched his sentences of atonement. Standing alone on the crest of the hill, Stringer believed himself at peace. He was safe in enemy territory. There was no evidence of stealth, or of conflict or violence. It

had been years since he'd heard explosions. The authorities forbade them to talk of the war, and he'd managed
to erase many of the things that he'd seen and done,
thanks to the condition of his life. He believed, without
any evidence for it, that he and Steinberg were necessary
to each other. In that way the future was secured.

After a time Stringer walked down the hill to join his
friend, and they would sit for a while at opposite ends of
the same log, Steinberg with his past, and Stringer with
his memory.